# BRANDED

# M. E. ALLEN

*Branded* was written by the mother-and-son writing partnership of Eleanor and Max Allen.

Eleanor Allen has written many books for young adults. She lives in Worcester.

Max Allen is a university student, dividing his time (and losing track of his possessions) between London, Worcester and Surrey.

# BRANDED

## M.E. ALLEN

EGMONT

Thanks to Cally and Emma, Lesley and
Linda for support and encouragement.


First published in Great Britain 2002
by Egmont Books Limited
239 Kensington High Street
London W8 6SA

Text copyright © 2002 M.E. Allen
Cover design copyright © 2002 Egmont Books Ltd

The moral rights of the authors have been asserted

ISBN 0 7497 4636 X

10 9 8 7 6 5 4 3 2 1

A CIP catalogue record for this title
is available from the British Library

Typeset by Avon DataSet Ltd, Bidford on Avon B50 4JH
Printed and bound in Great Britain
by Cox & Wyman Ltd, Reading, Berkshire

# CONTENTS

# Prologue

# If you can, I can

'*What-t*!' I splutter. 'A *girlfriend* – YOU? Ha!'

I mime splitting my sides.

'Yeah.' Ric growls. 'And here's the email evidence.'

I read the message out loud. I put on a girlie-type lisp and flutter my eyelashes.

Bunny, can't wait to see you in August.
Lurve, Carrot-top.

'Oooo-er!' I chortle. ' "Bunny", "Carrot-top". What's all that rot?'

Ric smirks. 'She says my nose twitches like a rabbit's when I'm nervous.'

Would you *believe* he'd admit that?

I turn my hands into a rabbit's ears and wriggle my nose.

But Ric just grins this ugly, smug grin.

'So what's with the Carrot-top? Confess!'

' 'Cos her nickname's Carro – short for Caroline. Carro – Carrot-top. And bunnies eat carrots. Geddit?'

'That is *so* sick-making.'

I stagger over to his wastepaper basket and pretend to puke into it.

'Knew you'd be jealous.'

'Jealous, *me?* Like I care! Don't start me off laughing again. I might bust my gut. Picture it – exploded gut all over your bedroom.'

'Who'd have thought *I'd* be the first of us to get a girlfriend,' he chortles. He's, like, *really* rubbing it in.

'Any idiot can get a girlfriend,' I sneer. 'You've just proved it. Specially one who must be blind, deaf and colour-blind. Oh, yeah – *and* lost her sense of smell. Quality's what counts.'

'Oh yeah?'

'Yeah!'

'I've gorra girlfriend,' chants Ric. 'And you haven't. And there's nothing wrong with her neither. So put that in your pipe an' smoke it!'

And he starts preening himself. Like he's just been awarded his half-colours for soccer and I haven't. And we both know I can mickey-take as much as I like, underneath, I *am* gutted.

Okay, so Ric only met this stupid girl-person for an hour on a cross channel ferry two days ago, during spring half-term. Okay, so she lives miles away. A place we've never even heard of. The fact is, she's emailing him and texting him. Fact is, she says she's getting her parents to bring her down here to visit him. In the school holidays. In August.

No point claiming she doesn't qualify.

My best mate's got a girlfriend.

I haven't.

Fourteen years old and I've never had a girlfriend.

'Girlfriends?' I fling. 'Who needs 'em? I could pull any time I like. Just haven't gotten around to it yet.'

'Oh yeah?'

'Yeah! And if I did, I'd make sure she was here – on the spot. Not at the ends of the earth, like yours, you great dork.'

'Oh yeah?'

'Yeah! And there's this saying, about a bird in the hand being worth two in the bush. Know what that means? It means, a girl in your home town's worth TWO on the Internet.'

'Oh yeah?'

'Yeah!'

'OK – *prove* it. You reckon you're so sexy – get a girl to go out with you. Before Carro comes. Before

August. Otherwise, you're nothing but a loud-mouthed LOSER!'

'That a challenge?'

'What's it sound like?'

'OK then – you're on.'

Help!

What've I *done?*

# Chapter 1

# Is my label showing?

# Getting into gear

It's the following morning – Saturday – and my mobile's ringing.

Brrring-brrring, brrring-brrring . . .

Dad pokes his head round my door. 'Wake up and answer that, you lazy prat.'

Feebly I raise my head off the pillow. I reach out a shaky hand. I clutch the phone to my ear. I try to say 'hello', but my mouth's too dry. A croak comes out.

'Hi,' mutters a flat, dull voice. ''s Ric.'

I detach my tongue from the roof of my mouth. 'Oh – yeah. Wha'?'

'Going into town. Need new clothes. Want to come?'

'Sorry, can't. Got no dosh.'

'OK. Right. See ya.'

Click. He's gone.

Fifteen seconds exactly. Typical. It's his mum's fault. She reads their phone bill like it's horror fiction – eyes popping, hand clutching throat. A five minute call to my mobile and it could be a fatal heart attack scenario.

Brrring-brrring, brrring-brrring . . .

'Hel-lo. What now?' I snarl.

Only it's not Ric ringing back. It's a girl's voice. All bouncing and up and at 'em, like the voice-over on my mum's aerobics video. It's my old mate Sandi.

'You up yet?' it demands.

''Course!' (Indignant) 'What you take me for?'

'A lazy prat. Going to the disco tonight?'

Pause. I'm struggling to crank-start my brain.

'Er – disco?'

'At St Thomas's Church Hall, dumbo. Becky's only been selling tickets all week. In aid of Save The Panda.'

'Er, um – which Becky's that?'

'The new girl.'

'Ah, *that* Becky . . .'

Hmmm . . . I quite fancy that Becky, as a matter of fact. Wonder if this could be my chance to have a crack at Ric's challenge. I've got nine weeks to win it, but got to start the girlfriend caper some time . . .

'So ARE you going?'

'Er . . .'

'Tickets still available on the door. Two quid a go and extra for refreshments. Ric's coming.'

'Oh – er . . .' Wonder if I'd be aiming too high with Becky?

'Antisocial!' Sandi flings.

'*What?*'

'YOU!'

'I am NOT!'

'So why're you not coming? Everybody else is.'

'*Everybody*?'

'Yeah.'

An interesting thought pops into my brain. Wonder if Becky herself's put Sandi up to ringing me? Girls do that sorta thing. Getting each other to ring up boys they fancy. Yeah, p'raps Becky fancies me.

'Well I didn't say I *wasn't* coming, did I?'

'Oh.' (Slight softening of tone.) 'So I'll see you there, then?'

Pause. 'Could be . . .'

'Give me a straight yes or no.'

'OK, then. Yeah. See ya.'

'Right – I'll see ya.'

A second or two later, I'm out of bed and flinging open my wardrobe. What to wear to the disco? What would impress Becky?

My wardrobe's stuffed so full, it won't shut

properly. I start rooting through the hanging stuff. An old anorak; track suit from when I was nine; tank top Mum bought me one day when she was out of her mind; T-shirt with Power Rangers on it . . . Waste of time.

All stuff in current use is piled in the bottom.

I start pulling it out. Crumpled, smelling of stale socks . . . Oh no! Where have all my clothes gone? Where's the stuff I carried home in all those shiny boutique bags? Items I've admired myself in from every possible angle in the mirrors inside those wardrobe doors.

Rags. Out-of-fashion RAGS.

My eye flickers over a pale blue T-shirt. I hold it up. Not bad. If washed by Mum immediately, time for it to dry. Ironed and sprayed with plenty of fabric freshener, not bad. Not *too* bad . . .

Arrrgh! I wore it as mufti on Red Nose Day last month. Crisis. Becky'll think I'm a one T-shirt kid.

I kick the shirt back into the wardrobe. The other stuff I leave on the floor.

I'm back on the phone.

'Hi – Ric? Er – think I will come into town.'

'Oh – acquired the moulah?'

'Not yet, but I'm on to it. Meet you at the bus station in an hour? OK. See ya.'

## Dishing no dosh

I corner the parents in the kitchen.

'Dad, I need some dosh.'

Dad turns from the window and eyes me like I'm the answer to his prayers. 'Mow that lawn, son, and it's a deal.'

'Er – I mean *real* dosh. Need a new T-shirt.'

His face falls. He shakes his head and backs away, raising his hands in a gesture of neutrality. 'Better ask your mum, then.'

'Mu-um, can 'ave a new T-shirt?'

My mum stands her ground. 'You had new trainers last week.'

'Trainers go on your feet,' I explain. 'I've nothing to wear on my top.'

'Rubbish! You've loads of stuff.'

'There's this disco . . . I need something *special* . . .'

'And I'm not paying for discos, either. That comes out of your pocket money.'

'But my money's all stashed away in my Flying Fund.'

Mum shrugs.

'You don't expect me to rifle my Flying Fund, d'you?'

Mum shrugs again.

I turn and appeal to Dad. 'Thought you *wanted* me to be a pilot . . .'

Dad just copies Mum's shrug.

'I'm not paying for the disco,' Mum repeats. 'And your wardrobe's stuffed to the eyeballs with T-shirts. So just be said!'

'What?' I groan and screw up my face like Jeremy Paxman. 'Was that a metaphor you just used? Or was it personification?'

Ooops! My mum does not appreciate me showing off my English Language skills. Time to beat a hasty retreat.

'I'll end up a saddo loner, standing on the touch-line of life,' I fling, as I slam the kitchen door (I can do imagery). 'Or a lavatory attendant,' I shout through the crack. 'Or both! And it'll be all my parents' fault!'

# Downtown blues

Return bus fare, plus hamburger and Coke to stave off hunger-pangs while browsing, have already taken a chunk out of my Flying Fund. And Ric and I've not even left the bus station.

Two hours later, we're downing Cokes again. Ric's got two carrier bags. He's looking smug. His mum gave him enough moulah to get himself a T-shirt *and* a pair of jeans. Bully for him.

I've bought nothing, so far.

To be honest, I don't envy Ric. I wouldn't be seen dead in what he's chosen. Everybody's got the same. In that T-shirt, with those jeans, Ric'll not stand out.

But I want to stand out. Tonight, when I walk into that church hall, I intend to knock 'em cold. What I'm looking for is a T-shirt that, when I put it on, *transforms* me.

'Seen nothing yet, then?' Ric asks. He's smothering a yawn.

'Nah.'

He's also got himself a sandwich. I've decided to do without. The price is sheer daylight robbery. I've said I'm not hungry, but my stomach's making noises like there's a cat trapped inside, and there's this kid in a pushchair at the next table who's giving me some very funny looks. I try a bit of muscle-clenching, to nil effect.

I can see Ric's battery's running flat. He's got his gear. Now he'd really like to be off home. I glance at my watch. Only an hour's shopping time left before we catch the bus. Ric's arranged for his mum to pick him up from our house at four o'clock.

'Can't you gerra move on? You're eating (joke) into my shopping time.'

Ric opens up his sandwich and inspects the filling. He takes out a slice of cucumber with finicky fingers and places it on the side of his plate. 'Always makes me belch, cucumber.' He carefully reconstructs the sandwich, like it's a work of art. Then he starts slowly chewing his way through it.

I sit eyeing my watch and tapping my foot. I'd like to ram the sandwich down his throat.

'That slice of cucumber cost you twenty pence. At least.' I pick it up and eat it. 'D'you realize the cost of that sandwich could've fed a whole Third World family for a week?'

'What's bugging you?'

'Nothing. Let's go.'

I spring up from the table and head for the door.

Ric stuffs the remains of the sandwich into his mouth. He snatches up his carrier bags and trails after me, muttering and complaining.

## Big spender

We're in the most up-market department store in town, both reeking of freebie squirts of designer eau de toilette. Great bottles. Pity about the smell. More like Eau de Toilet. Phaugh! We stink like a couple of Premier Division footballers on a night out.

I'm wandering around fingering things. Unimpressed.

'How about this?' says Ric. He's holding up a blue polo shirt with an animal motif on the left breast. 'They've got it in Small.'

I cock my head and inspect it. 'Mmm, not bad . . .'

Hopeful look above the T-shirt.

'But boring. Everybody's got one.'

'I've not,' says Ric. He rolls his eyes and hangs it

back on the rack. He mutters something that sounds like 'underpants' and wanders off on his own.

It's then, as a last resort, that I'm drawn into this exclusive boutique, just round the corner from the department store. It's there that I finally spot it. The T-shirt of my dreams. And it's in my size!

I pull it off the rack and soak up the details. A dark blue polymide and lycra mix. Slightly fitted, with arms cut slightly shorter and slightly tighter than normal. It's the 'slightly' that makes it. The whole cut reeks of class. Wow! It speaks to me. 'Buy me . . .' it seems to urge. 'Buy me . . .' The label's black and white and sports a hologram. It's a D & G. I flick the label over and a shudder runs through me as I spot the price. But *worth* it, I say to myself. Worth every blessed penny. In fact, the price makes it even more wannahave.

'Can I help you?' asks the assistant. You can tell from his snooty tone he doesn't mean that. What he means is, quit fingering stuff you can't afford and the Exit's over there.

'Er – I'd like to try this on,' says a voice. Mine. Have I gone mad?

The assistant frowns. He gives me the once over,

letting me know he'll be keeping an eye on me. I follow him to a cubicle. He draws the stiff, white curtain around me.

What am I *doing*? He's right, I can't afford this. That Eau de Toilet must've gone to my head.

My hand's shaking as I slip the T-shirt off its hanger. Actually I do have enough in my Flying Fund to cover it, I tell myself. I really could buy it.

Oh yes. YESS! Do I feel good, or do I feel good. I love myself so much in this, I'd have the nerve to chat up every babe in town. Ric's challenge would be a cinch. I rotate my hips like a Brazilian footballer who's just scored. Phwoar! Becky, you might get crushed in the stampede.

Woah! Get a grip. Think about your future. Buy this and your entire Flying Fund will have flown.

I glance at my watch. Less than half an hour before we have to catch the bus. What else will I find in half an hour that'll satisfy me, after this? Beads of sweat appear on my forehead.

I feel something itching me. It's the inside label. I look at it. DRY CLEAN ONLY. Oh heck. What would my mum say about a T-shirt that needed dry cleaning? She'd kill me.

'Any good?' asks the shop assistant bloke, checking up on me.

'Er . . .' I shake my head. 'It says dry clean . . .'

'Oh, no problem.' He's staring over the top of my head as he's talking. Like I'm not worth his full attention. 'If you turn them inside out and wash by hand in cold water, they're fine,' he trots out.

'Oh? Really?'

'I do it all the time. No problem.'

It feels like a weight's lifted off my shoulders. That solves that, then. No need to dry clean. Everything else goes right out of my mind.

'I'll take it,' I say breathlessly. 'I'll take it. Only I've just got to pop and withdraw the cash. Can you put it aside for me?'

Ten minutes later, the T-shirt's mine. Clutching the bag with shaking hands, I go back into the department store in search of Ric. I track him down in the underwear section. He's clicking his tongue over the price of Calvin Klein boxers. A rip-off, he says, compared to what his mum pays for his at Marks and Spencer.

His face lights up when he sees the bag. 'Got something at last?'

'You bet!' I say. 'This piece of designer gear's pure babe-magnet, mate. Tonight, with this on – I'll be fighting 'em off. Come on, let's go.'

## Near disasterville

Mum eyes the name on my carrier bag as we walk in. She raises her eyebrows. She puts on an expression like a constipated ostrich. 'Greetings, Big Spender. Could the Flying Fund *really* afford that?'

'Wait till you see it,' I mutter. 'Worth every penny.'

'I bet pennies didn't enter into it,' she frowns.

I dash upstairs to preen myself in private, leaving Ric to the tender mercies of my mum.

The top feels like a million dollars. I don't regret buying it. No way. It puts me in a different league. Everything else I own is rubbish, compared to this. I kick the crumpled, fetid rubbish aside. I view the new, improved me from every angle before I'm ready to go down and show myself off.

'Well, what d'you think?'

'Very nice, dear.'

'Very NICE?'

'Bit tight, though, isn't it?'

'It's FITTED, Mum! This is quality couture design!'

I appeal to Ric. 'Doesn't this just shriek CLASS to you?'

'Yeah,' says Ric. He nods his head, like one of those dogs in the back of a car. 'Yeah.'

Strewth – that's got a girlfriend, and I haven't. Is there no justice in this world? Still, after tonight, justice will be done. 'Cos with this T-shirt on I feel irresistible.

'Fancy a Coke?'

'Yeah. Ta.'

We head for the kitchen.

'Shouldn't you take that new top off till you're ready to go out?' Mum lobs after me.

I sigh and ignore her. My mum is so embarrassing. She even buys supermarket brand Coke by the litre bottle. Anything to save a penny or two. Everything I buy's going to be top of the range from now on.

I apologize for the Coke and get out two of Dad's beer glasses. 'Cos I'm feeling good, I start larking around. Ric joins in. Next thing I know, the stupid fat-head thinks it's funny to shake up the Coke bottle. Well, I'll spare you all the sordid details. The worst that could happen, happens. Coke straight down the front of my D & G!

I reel backwards against the kitchen table. 'I don't be-lieve it!' I yell.

'Stop flapping around like a headless chicken and get it under the cold tap, quick!' yells Ric.

I rush up to the bathroom, hyperventilating. I whip off my precious T-shirt and dangle it under the cold tap. I examine the liquid as it flows down the plug hole. Brown. Might just not be the end of the world.

I take the T-shirt into my bedroom. I put it on a hanger by the open window and examine it again. The only stain I can see looks like a wet stain. Hallelujah!

Ric might still be alive when his mum collects him, after all.

## Dolce and Gabbana-d

Half-past six. Time to start getting ready for the disco.

A quick shower, then I pad back to my room. I

put on a CD and psyche myself up with a John Travolta routine. Pretty cool, if I do say so myself. Becky, are you ready for this?

I take hold of the Dolce & Gabbana and start to dance with it. Urrgh! It's still damp on the front. I look at my watch. 6.45pm. Crisis!

I run a hand through my hair. I moan.

Then inspiration strikes. Iron. Iron it dry.

Somebody's left the ironing board set up on the landing from an earlier session. I click on the iron. I place the T-shirt in position. Then I pop into the bathroom for a facial inspection, while the iron's heating up.

The dab of spot remover I used earlier on my chin's worked, but they should warn you it removes the skin as well. I root out a tube of Mum's tinted foundation cream and smooth a blob of that over. I do my hair at the same time. I've got it down to a fine art. First wet hair, then towel dry. Now apply a spot of gel to the fingers. Run through hair and shake vigorously.

I rush back to the T-shirt and grab the iron. But the minute the iron touches the T-shirt, I know I have trouble. The iron won't slide. The regulator's been left on high, I whip it off again, double quick. Too late!

DISASTERVILLE!

A great wedge-shape has burnt itself into the fabric. You can even see three round dots where the steam holes were.

'What can I do, Mum?' I wail. I sound like a three year old who's broken the head off his Action Man. But old habits die hard.

'Nothing,' she says. 'You've really gone and Dolce & Gabbana-d it, haven't you?' She laughs at her own feeble joke. At a time like this!

'What'll I do?' I groan. 'I've got nothing else to wear!'

'Try tucking it into your trousers,' she says. 'That way, it'll hardly show.'

'Tucked in's not COOL,' I yell. 'How much does it show? Go on – tell me. Be honest.'

'Well, I can see it if I look. But I don't suppose your friends will be looking all that closely, will they?'

That is NOT what I want to hear. My own mother and she just doesn't understand. This beautiful, astronomically expensive item on which I've squandered my entire Flying Fund is ruined. How can I feel good? How can I impress a girl and win the challenge with a wedge shape complete with steam holes that shouts HOT IRON, smack in the middle of my front?

Ric couldn't have done a better sabotage job if he'd tried.

## No go with logo

St Thomas's Church Hall. 7.30pm.

This is the biz. Thumping disco music, heat, lights, dancing, crowds of friends. I'm sitting at one of the tables down the side of the hall with a few of my mates. Becky's sitting opposite me, drinking Diet Coke.

And to think, after my disaster with the T-shirt, I nearly didn't come.

My eyes flicker away from Becky to check the D & G situation. This place is as hot and close as a giant's armpit. My lower half's hidden by the table, so I'm wondering if I can now untie the sweater that's knotted with cunning casualness around my waist. Nah. Not yet. I'll wait till I'm up and dancing before I risk it.

Becky's wearing grey. Understated. That's her style. I think it suits her.

I'm certain she fancies me. Definitely. YES! She might even ask *me* out, if I play my cards right.

She's a great talker. Really earnest. Fantastic range of subjects. It's a shame I can't catch everything she's saying, 'cos of the music. I'm sure its all really interesting stuff.

I lean across the table. I cup my ear and nod wisely. 'I agree,' I say. 'Yeah, I agree. Seals? Oh, yes. Whales? Yeah – 'course . . . Sellafield? Definitely. I support them all. Definitely. Always been a big Sellafield supporter.'

'You SUPPORT SELLAFIELD?'

I've pressed the wrong button here. Can see that from the two points of horror that were her eyes. Funny, wouldn't have had Becky down as a football supporter.

'Well, 'course, I'm a big Man United fan as well.' I mutter. 'Chelsea? Arsenal? Aston Villa?'

'Sellafield's a nuclear power station, you brainless PRAT!' shrieks Sandi. 'Don't you ever watch the news?'

'Can't you spot a JOKE when you hear one?' I shout back.

Gaff cleverly covered, I think. Must remember to hold a grudge against Sandi, though.

Don't know what's gotten into Sandi tonight. She's being a real grump.

I've been avoiding Ric, 'cos I hold him to blame for the whole D & G disaster, and I might still decide to kill him. But at this minute, he finally corners me.

'How's the you-know-what?' he shouts. Typical subtlety. 'Did it stain?'

'It's fine,' I mutter, out of the corner of my mouth.

He grabs a stool. He starts to work it into a space at our table that doesn't exist. I spot trouble looming.

'Hey, what's this for, then?' He reaches across and playfully tweaks one of the arms of the sweater.

'Cut it out.' I knock his hand away. I've got a smile pinned to my face, but I trust he's picked up the warning note in my voice. NASA to Outer Space – are you receiving me?

He gives me a nudge. He leers. 'I see you're talking to Bec-ky, hey? Hey? Gonna ask her out? Hey?'

I cringe. I lean forward to cut him out. 'What were you saying, Becky?'

'Like his T-shirt, do you?' Ric's leaning across the table as well. 'I was with him when he bought it. *I* know what he paid for it.'

While I'm dithering over whether to kick the stool from under him or strangle the prat, he tells her. Straight out.

Actually, she's impressed. Her eyes gape open. But I've got this uneasy feeling. Like when Ric once pushed me off the high diving board and I wasn't sure how I was going to hit the water.

'You really paid *that* much?'

'Yeah,' I shrug.

'WHY?'

The word whizzes across the table like a dart, aimed straight at my conscience. Wow – have I belly-flopped. Big time.

'The cut . . .' I mutter. 'The logo . . . Everything . . .'

'You'd pay all that – just for a *logo*?'

She makes logo sound like a dirty word.

'Yeah – it makes me feel good.'

I wriggle my shoulders inside the T-shirt. I could do with a shot of that feel-good right now. Come on, do your magic for me, you beautiful polymide and lycra-mix baby. Zilch. Becky's withering stare's shrivelled up all the pizzazz. I might as well be wearing a dishcloth. I finger the arms of the sweater. I'm checking they're still covering the scorch mark. If the scorch mark got revealed on top of this, it would *kill* me.

'Pathetic,' Becky hisses. 'I didn't have you down as a label-junkie.'

'Wha-*t*?' I can't *be-lieve* what she just called me.

'Label-junkie. Pathetic. Don't you know half the world's starving?'

Yeah. I'm the one that goes around telling morons like Ric that. And, what's more, the only reason I bought this flipping T-shirt was to impress *her*. There *is* no justice in the world.

My mouth's gone dry. My brain's seized up. I can't think of anything clever or witty to say. The wound's too deep.

'There's no need to be so personal . . .' That's all I can mumble. Pathetic. Should have kept my mouth shut.

'Ooops – Becky doesn't go in for logos,' Ric points out. He's grinning.

'Butt out!'

Becky's got this expression on her face. Like she's revolted. Like I'm a worm that's just crawled out of her salad.

Suddenly, there's this voice in my head. It's whispering that 'praps I'm not the one that's pathetic. P'raps she is. She's just totally rubbished me. Destroyed any bit of magic left in my beautiful T-shirt. She's a killjoy, that's what she is. Right now, she doesn't look as good as I thought. In fact, that grey outfit's downright frumpy.

'No logos on Becky,' I hiss. My voice sounds really sneery.

Somebody echoes me. 'No logos on Becky!' Everybody round the table starts laughing.

It's not all that funny. OK, it's not funny at all. But everybody's in the sort of mood where they'd laugh at anything. If I stood on top of my stool and shouted, 'Toilet tissue', I'd get a reputation for being witty.

Becky's not laughing, though, she's got two fiery spots on her cheeks. I have a feeling I've got my own back.

# No friend of mine

O-oh! Ric's just noticed me fumbling with the sleeves of my sweater again. He's looking suspicious. He makes a grab at one. This time I bring up my knee to fend him off. Fatal.

My knee bashes against the table and Becky gets her Diet Coke smack in her lap. All over the pale grey skirt. She lets out a yelp and leaps up, like she's just been groped. You can't help noticing it's soaked through to the back of her skirt as well.

'You look like you've wet yourself,' laughs Sandi.

I try to apologize to Becky. I really do. But I can't keep my face straight.

It's obvious she would like to kill me.

'Come to the loos.' Natasha's trying to smooth things over. 'Bring a stool to stand on. Come and help, Sandi. We'll stick her under the handdrier.'

'I'll get you another Coke,' I titter.

After I've got the Coke, I head for the loos myself. Arrrgh! My hair's collapsed in the heat. It's lying flat on my head, like it's been splattered there by a low-flying cow. I spend a few minutes wetting it and trying to coax it back into shape. Then I root through my pockets. A two pound coin and a handful of small change. That's all that's left from my Flying Fund.

Becky's still not reappeared. Neither have Sandi and Natasha. I thirstily eye Becky's Coke. It might go to waste, so I drink it myself. Only I start to feel guilty. Don't want to get a reputation for being mean. Then I come up with this really clever idea. I write SORRY on the back of a coaster and go to shove it under the door of the girls' loos.

I put my ear to the door. I can hear Becky, Sandi and Natasha squawking inside. A lot of girlie-bonding's going on. Sounds like they're having more fun than they were in the disco. Then I overhear a very *rude* comment about myself. I'm not going to repeat it. But from now on, Sandi's no longer a friend of mine.

I'm tempted to bang the door open and shout '*Boo*!' Vivid scenes of girlie panic flicker through my mind. But I fight it. Instead, I post the coaster under the door, as planned.

I think that's very generous of me, considering the circumstances.

# Gross ingratitude

Everybody else still seems to be having a wild time at the disco. But my chances of getting a date with Becky are now as Dolce & Gabanna-d as the T-shirt. I pull the two quid coin out of my pocket and flick it thoughtfully. I can either stay and blow it on more Coke and crisps. Or I can head for home while I've still got something left to start new savings.

I slip out of the hall and head for home. I fill my lungs with refreshing night air and stare up at the stars. Sometimes you can't beat a bit of your own company. I notice it's turned chilly, so I untie the sweater and put it on. Glad I've got it, actually.

That Becky. Fancy her not being my type, after all. Probably spends her time watching *Channel Four News*, *Wildlife On One*, or knitting blankets for refugees. Me, I think there's room in life for a bit of colour. A bit of recklessness. You have to branch out sometimes. Be bold.

Still, this is a bit of a dud ending to what was supposed to be a great night out. My Flying Fund's flown; I've not a decent rag to my name; the girl I fancied my chances of going out with hates me and

I've not won the challenge. And if Ric comes anywhere near me, I'll *kill* him.

I turn down the High Street. Suddenly, I hear footsteps running behind me. I whip around. It's Sandi, of all people.

'What're you doing here, Sand?' I glower. (I've not forgotten what she said about me in the loos.)

'You dropped something.' She holds out a two pound coin.

'What?' I dive a hand into my pocket. I rummage around. Nothing there but small change. How could I have been so careless? If I'd got home and discovered I'd even lost my last two quid, that'd have chewed me up good and proper.

'Thanks, Sandi. You're a pal.'

I snatch the coin out of her hand.

Then, in sheer gratitude, I scoop the loose change out of my pocket. I hold it out to her. 'Here, buy yourself some crisps.'

Does she smile and say thank you? Or even, 'S'okay, I've already pigged three packets'?

NO.

Know what she does? She kicks me. Would you

believe that? She kicks me so hard on the shin, she bruises me.

And she doesn't say a word. No explanation. Nothing. She just tosses her head, about turns, and stalks off.

Mamma mia! What was all that about?

Girls. After tonight – forget 'em.

The challenge is off.

Girls spell nothing but TROUBLE.

# Chapter 2
# Showdown at
# the barbi

# Sarah's inviting

Just a day or two after Becky's Save The Panda disco fiasco, I'm off games with a babe called Sarah. The rest of our set are late getting changed back and fate throws us together early, outside Modern Languages 2.

I'm pretending to study this poster of the Alps, when suddenly she speaks to me.

'Liked the T-shirt you had on the other night,' she says. 'Très chic.' And she flashes me this really nice smile.

'Merci,' I gulp. 'Merci beaucoup.'

And it feels, like really cool. Talking in French *outside* the French room. And being paid a compliment by Sarah. 'Cos Sarah's got brilliant taste. Everybody says so. She's *really* confident and efficient and got-together. She's all clean and pressed and polished. She wears her school uniform like she's proud of it. And she's brilliant at languages.

Sarah starts telling me she wants to be an interpreter. I tell her I bet she'd be really good at it. Then I tell her I want to be a pilot. And she says 'Wow!' and looks mega impressed.

Well, next thing I know, she's inviting me to her barbecue this Sunday. The one she's having to welcome her French pen friend who's coming over on a private exchange. And she says she'll invite Ric as well, 'cos he's my mate. Really thoughtful. She's like that.

Well, don't know how *you'd* 'interpret' this, but to my mind (and I've given it loadsa thought) she's signalling that she fancies me.

Yup. Sarah. Thought she was way out of my league.

Yeah, yeah . . . I know! I know! I said girls were nothing but trouble. I said the challenge was off.

But that was before *Sarah* came into my life.

P'raps when you start looking at girls, like you're interested in them, they start looking at you back. P'raps that's the trick.

Anyway, the challenge is definitely back on and I can't wait for Sunday.


## Salad tosser

'Hi. Speak to Ric, please?'

I've got Ric's dad on the line. 'Nice timing,' he says. 'As usual. His mum's just this minute put his dinner on the table.'

'Oh. Can you get him to ring me back when he's finished, then?'

I'm just putting the receiver down. But Ric's dad's still bawling something. 'Er – what?'

'If *he* rings *you* back, that goes on *our* bill. So he'd better speak to you now, while it's going on *yours*. You can speak for one minute. I repeat, ONE minute. Or his dinner will go cold.'

I can hear Ric stomping towards the phone. And I can hear his mum's voice shouting in the background.

'What?' hisses Ric. 'Make it snappy.' He sounds like he's wearing a bullet-proof vest and commentating from a war zone.

'Er – Sarah said she was going to invite you to her barbecue. The one she's having for her French exchange.'

'She already has. That all?'

'Er – how're you getting there?'

'My mum, I expect. Only she doesn't know it yet.'

'Can I scrounge a lift?'

''Spect so. Anything else? My shepherd pie's going cold.'

'Er – you taking anything?'

'Like what?'

'Er – well, thought I might take a potato salad.'

Scornful laugh. 'A *wha*'? Nah. Shouldn't think we need to take anything.'

'OK. Just checking. Enjoy the shepherd's –'

Click. He's gone.

Shame about the potato salad. I've just been watching this cookery programme on the telly, showing you how to do one. The chef said it was dead easy, just the thing for us guys to have a bash at to impress the ladies. I pictured taking one to the barbecue in a nice dish. Bet Sarah would've been impressed. But I can't risk being the only one who's taking something. Might as well arrive carrying a sign saying, 'I'm after you, Sarah.'

I treat myself to a good lie-in on Sunday morning. Need to be at my fresh-and-crispiest for Sarah. Then a nice shower and a few squirts of Dad's Armani under the armpits and across the chest. Like to smell it drifting up through the neck of my T-shirt (very confidence-boosting). Back to my room. I'm just putting the finishing touches to my hair when Ric rings.

'We'll pick you up at 2 o'clock. Don't keep us waiting.'

'OK.'

'What're you taking?'

'Nothing – like we agreed.'

'Er – I'm taking a potato salad.'

'*What*? I thought we agreed –'

'Changed my mind. My mum said it was a good idea.'

'But *I was doing a potato salad*!'

'Not much point having two. See ya at 2 o'clock. Be ready. Ciao!'

If somebody attached a power cable to me at this minute, I'd generate enough electricity to light up Old Trafford, The Millennium Stadium and the flipping Stade de France!

If I had Ric in front of me, no prizes for guessing what I'd do with his pathetic potato salad!

# Checkmate

'Looking for anything special?' asks my mum. She looks up from the Sunday papers and frowns. She's got the papers spread all over the kitchen table.

I'm rooting through the fridge.

'Need something for the barbecue.'

'I thought you said you weren't taking anything.'

'Ric's changed his mind.' I grind my teeth. 'He's pinched my idea. Now *he's* taking a potato salad. And why is our fridge two thirds *empty*?' I add. My voice squeaks accusingly.

'I think you'll find there's a packet of sausages in there, somewhere,' mumbles Mum.

I extract the sausages. I hold them up between my finger and thumb. Pale pink, like bloodless fingers. Tightly wrapped in cellophane. Stamped with yesterday's sell-by date.

'D'you seriously think I can turn up carrying these?'

Mum squints over her glasses. 'A few extra sausages are always welcome at a barbecue, but if you'd prefer something that's a bit more of a treat, I've got some chocolates in the cupboard. It was

Buy One, Get One Free. You can have the free ones.'

I slam the fridge door shut. I'm seething. 'You don't take chocolates to a barbecue.'

'They'd make a pleasant change, after all that meat.'

'N-O!'

Mum sighs and reaches for her coffee cup. I see her eyes drifting back to the newspapers. This annoys me even more.

Can't she see her son's having a crisis here?

I stomp towards the food cupboard. I fling it open and scan the shelves. The chocolates are there. Sitting smugly among half-empty cereal packets, tins of Cling peaches and packets of Weight-Watchers' soups. I'm cursed with a mother from the Instant-Deep-Freeze-Oven-Ready-Boil-In-The-Bag-Microwave generation. When she watches cookery programmes on the telly, it's just for entertainment. No wonder I've been harbouring thoughts of abandoning my flying ambitions in favour of becoming a celebrity chef. And the girls go mad for TV chefs.

'Strawberries!' Mum's got a triumphant look on

her face. Like she's just called Bingo. 'Who can resist strawberries?'

I catch the cupboard door on half slam.

'Where'd I get them?'

'Supermarket's open.'

I glance at my watch. The supermarket's a good drive away. But we'd just have time. If we set off like – NOW.

I'm dashing indoors, carrying a bag containing two family-size punnets of huge, succulent-looking strawberries. Out of the corner of my eye, I spot Ric's mum's car. It's just turning into our street. Not a minute to spare.

I'm not going to hand the strawberries over to Sarah in their pre-packed state. Complete with labels showing what a rip-off price we've paid for them. Oh no.

While Mum's chatting to Ric's mum, I dash into the back garden. I tear leaves off our grapeless vine. Then I run to the kitchen and grab a round, rustic-looking bread basket. I line it with the leaves, then I carefully pile in the strawberries.

Voila! They look hand-picked. Excellent! I

kiss my fingers, Gary Rhodes fashion.

'Yummy,' says Ric's mum. I'm cradling the basket on my lap on the back seat of the car. 'Those look good.'

Next to me on the seat sits Ric's clingfilm covered salad. It's sweating slightly in the heat. I run an expert's eye over it. Rough lumps of potato in what looks like bought mayonnaise. Yuck!

Ric's looking round from the passenger seat. He's eyeing my strawberries and he seems really cheesed off.

As we drive off to the barbecue, I lounge back and flash him a modest smile.

## Strawberry fields, never

'How thoughtful, boys,' gushes Sarah's mum, when we hand over our culinary contributions.

'Oh – another potato salad,' mutters Sarah. 'Thanks.' She dumps Ric's salad right at the back of the cold buffet table. Doesn't even remove the clingfilm.

Her face lights up at my offering, though. 'Strawberries! Scrumptious!'

'Picked at dawn by my own fair hands,' I say. And I flash her a teasing smirk.

'Oh yeah?' chips in Sandi, who's helping. 'Did you remember to send me a postcard?'

'Er – what?'

'Where's the sun tan?'

'What?'

'Those are Spanish strawberries, you berk. Spanish. Pop over to the Costa Fruitica before breakfast, did you? Costa Packet at Tesco, more like.'

I hang on to my cool, just. Sandi and I've known each other since Year One in primary school. She reckons it gives her the right to take liberties. It doesn't.

Sarah makes a space for my strawberries smack in the centre of the table. But just as she's putting them down, Sandi reaches across. She makes a grab at the monster strawberry I've carefully placed on top. 'Hey – look at that whopper.'

I slap her hand away. 'When God was handing out dignity and manners, Sandi,' I hiss, 'you must've been doing a handstand against the playground wall. With your skirt over your ears.'

Sandi lets out a loud guffaw. Then she says

something really rude about me. Straight out. In front of Sarah and her mum. Not to mention Ric.

Know what they do? They laugh. All three of them.

I'm getting really fed up with being made the butt of girlie jokes. Especially Sandi's. I've still not forgiven her for what she said about me at the disco. There's too much of this Girl Power about. Us boys usually have the good manners to mutter things among ourselves. Or out of the side of our mouths. Or behind our hands. Not straight in yer face.

'Er – why don't you boys pop over to the barbecue and grab yourselves a hot dog?' says Sarah's mum.

## Parlez avec – qui?

Sarah's dad's doing the barbecuing. He's one of those big, out-going types. He's 'jollying' things up with one of those plastic aprons that have a fat lady's body on it. I nod at it. 'That's about the same level as Sandi's humour.'

'My dad's got one of those,' says Ric. 'I bought it him. For Christmas.'

'That figures.'

'Here – shove that in your mouth.' Ric thrusts a hot dog at me. Then he saunters off. I expect he's still smarting over the strawberries. Serves him right.

I've noticed this before. There's nothing like coming up with a brilliant and original idea for creating a friend-free zone.

I take a big bite out of my hot dog. Arrrgh! A lethal mix of scorching heat and English mustard attacks my palate from the centre of the cold, slightly stale roll.

'You OK?'

I blink through watering eyes. It's Sarah. My knees go all trembly.

'Phew – yeah – fine. Your dad makes a mean hot dog.'

She smiles. Then she hands me a Coke – in a glass. And there's ice and lemon in it. I notice that I'm the only one singled out to get one. Wow.

'Thanks.'

I eye her up over the Coke.

'Like your top,' I say.

'It's an Agnès B.'

'Kind of her to lend it you,' I quip.

'Fancy practising your French?'

'Hey, that sounds good.' I roll my eyes. 'Mais oui.' This is turning out better than my wildest dreams. Sarah's actually chatting me up. 'Any time, cherie.' I say. And I roll my 'r' like I was born in the shadow of the Eiffel Tower with a clove of garlic in my mouth.

'Great. See that boy who's standing over there?'

I focus on this greasy-haired kid. He looks sixteen. He's wearing a Calvin Klein T-shirt and there's a silver medallion dangling round his neck.

'Him?'

'That's Jean-Claude,' she says. And she throws him this gooey sort of look.

'Who he?'

'My French pen friend. He's from Marseilles. He's dying to practise his English, and since you're just hanging around on your own doing nothing, I'd like you to go over and talk to him. I've got to help Mummy, you see.'

Did I mishear her? Hanging around on my own,

doing nothing? Did she actually mean that the way it sounded? And talk to the French pen friend? Excuse me . . .

'You want me to go and talk to – *him*?' I gasp.

She shrugs. 'Yeah – you just said you wanted to practise your French.'

'I thought you meant with you.'

Sarah's eyes go as round as a couple of bus headlights. She gives me this amazed, wide-eyed stare. Then she claps her hand to her mouth and starts to giggle. 'Do me a favour,' she splutters.

And something inside me goes twang. I turn icy cold. Then all red and hot, like an over-heated lightbulb. It's the way she said it – 'Do me a favour,' – like somebody's just suggested she go kiss a toad.

'I said you 'cos I'm not confident enough to hold a conversation with some French kid I don't know,' I mutter. Like she's read me all wrong and I'm, like, really annoyed with her.

She looks a bit unsure. Then she wipes the scorn off her face, to be on the safe side. 'You can manage a few friendly words with Jean-Claude, can't you?' she flings.

'Like what?'

'How should I know? Whatever you boys talk about.' Suddenly there's this snappy note in her voice. 'Only . . .' She frowns. 'Not football. Make sure you keep right off football. He's very rude about English football.'

I peer across at the Frenchie. 'Don't think we've got anything in common,' I say huffily.

'Oh, you're so pathetic,' she groans. 'Weedy. So – so – *English*!'

Then she snatches the Coke out of my hand – very petty, considering I've nearly drunk it all anyway – and she stalks off.

Phew – have I just made a prize idiot of myself, or what? How could I have been that wrong about Sarah? I must be as good at reading girls' minds as I am at speaking French. I feel like crawling under a stone. Seems that's where all the girls think I belong.

## French exchange

I scout around the garden. But I can't see another soul to talk to, apart from Ric. That comment about me hanging around on my own's still stinging, though. So I decide to overlook Ric's mean attitude and let bygones be bygones.

'Hi, Ric. How you doin'?'

'Butt out.'

'What?'

'I said "butt out",' he hisses.

Now I notice he's with this pert little thing. She's wearing one of those frocks that look like underskirts. How come Ric, who's already got a girlfriend, gets to chat her up, while I'm expected to waste my time parleying with a *him* whose eyebrows look like two snails on a collision course?

'Being unfaithful are we?' I say in this sarky voice, so the girl can hear. 'Oo-oo – what would Carrot-top say?' And I turn my hands into a couple of ears. Only, suddenly, my hands stop waggling. I've just noticed this girl's holding a plastic dish – full of *my* strawberries. And what's more, Ric's stuffing his fat face out of an identical dish.

I shoot over to the cold buffet table. All that's left in my rustic basket are the vine leaves. Slightly wilted.

'Your strawberries were very popular,' giggles Sarah's mum. She brushes at a suspicious pink patch on her blouse.

'I thought they were for later. *After* the barbecue,' I gasp.

'Nobody could resist them. But there's still plenty of salad left. Help yourself. Look, here's Ric's potato salad, still untouched.'

I groan. 'No thanks.' I snatch up my mum's rustic basket and hide it under the table, just in case somebody takes a fancy to that as well. I glance at my watch. Still an hour to kill before Ric's mum's due to fetch us. What to do? Stand around like a saddo loner, or . . .

With a sigh, I stroll over to the French Exchange from Marseilles.

'Ça-va?'

His face lights up. He starts gabbling away at me. But at the speed he's going, I can't pick up a single word. He seems to think I can parley enough Français to hold a conversation. In actual fact, I'm in danger of being put down to Set B.

I shake my head. 'Je ne parle pas q'un peu,' I tell him.

'Ah.' He nods. He rolls his eyes skywards, like he's thinking 'Typical.'

'Okay,' he mutters. 'No problem. I understand English. But speak slowly please.'

'Oh . . . Er – good . . .'

Silence. He eyes me expectantly.

More silence. Starting to become embarrassing silence.

'Er . . . Nice day. It's stayed dry . . .'

He looks at me down his French nose. He dangles a hand and shakes it scornfully from his wrist. 'Ze English. All zey ev-er talks about is ze weazzer.'

'Er – fancy another hot dog – chien-chaud?' I say. To prove him wrong.

He shakes his head this time. He pants. He wafts his hand across his mouth, like it's on fire. Quite funny, actually.

'Yeah . . .' I join in and we laugh together.

'English cooking, eh? Bah!'

I stop laughing. 'Well not always,' I tell him. 'Pas toujours. Some of our top chefs are the best in the world these days.'

He stops laughing. He glowers at me from under

his snail-like eyebrows. '*English* chefs best in ze world?' he growls. 'You serious?'

'Yeah,' I nod. I start to lob names at him. 'Gary Rhodes, Ainsley Harriott, Rick Stein, Delia Smith. Er, Jamie Oliver –'

'Bah! English chefs *lousy*.'

'What?' I gasp.

'French cooking best in ze world.'

'Well, okay. Some of the best dishes do come from France,' I admit, thinking of the mouth-watering illustrations in Mum's *Round the World Cookbook* (an unused Christmas present from Dad). 'Like cassoulet, creme caramel, French onion soup, er, French dressing . . .'

'And what *English* dishes – hey? Le ros bif and le hot dog!'

I grit my teeth. 'Pas responsible pour le hot dog, c'est Americain, je pense. But there are some great English dishes.'

The French kid folds his arms across his chest. He rolls his eyes. 'Yeah-yeah, yeah-yeah . . .' he goes. I don't like his attitude, to be honest. All I'm doing is trying to make polite conversation, and all he wants to do is slag off English food and English chefs.

'What's more,' I grind out, 'I was watching this programme. It said us English, we cook dishes from all round the world these days. But you – you French, you can only cook French food.'

He screws up his eyes. 'Eh? Par-don?' I'm talking a bit fast by this time. He hasn't understood. Doesn't matter. He's only got one song to sing anyway.

'English cooking,' he says, 'is yuck.' He jabs a finger at my chest. 'Yuck, (jab), yuck (jab), yuck!'

I'm fast losing my cool here. Sarah prefers him – this finger-jabbing Frenchie – to me?

'Listen here, you prejudiced moron,' I hiss. I've said it before I can stop myself. But I said it fast and low. P'raps he won't have understood . . .

'Moron? You calling me *moron*?' he roars. (He would know that word, wouldn't he?)

Wow, is he mad. I take a step backwards. I can feel my knees starting to shake. But once I'm wound up, there's no stopping me. 'Yeah!'

He grabs me by the arm and hauls me across to the barbecue. He snatches up a couple of freshly made hot dogs and, while Sarah's dad stands looking puzzled, he opens them up and loads them with great dollops of mustard and ketchup. He squashes the tops down so the contents ooze down the sides. Then, as I'm standing there, like a prize twerp, wondering what he intends to do next, he lobs them at me.

First one. Then the other.

They hit me on the chest, then slide off, leaving a trail of mustard and ketchup. All down the front of my second-best T-shirt.

Let's get this clear. I'm not into violence. And I'm all for the Euro – I think. And Hands Across the World and all that sorta stuff. But let's face it, no ugly, English-girl-snatching, French-frog's going to cover my second-best T-shirt in mustard and ketchup and get away with it.

Now I'm striding across to the table. Now *I'm* snatching up the ketchup bottle.

I let him have it – straight down his shirt front.

He starts to grab finger rolls. He lobs them at me. He screams insults. 'Cochon! Rosbif! Margaret Thatcher!'

(I can hear screaming and shouting all around me. I take no notice.)

Now I'm marching over to the cold buffet table. I know exactly what I'm looking for. Ric's potato salad. I whip off the clingfilm. As the French pen friend charges up to me, I let him have it – smack in the kisser.

Suddenly my arms are pinned to my sides.

'Let go! Let me get at him!' I yell.

'Have you gone out of your tiny mind?' hisses Ric.

At the same time I can see Jean-Claude being grappled by Sarah.

Sarah's dad strides between us. His face looks all threatening, above the sexy pinny. There's a long-handled fork waving in his hand.

Sarah's all white-faced and furious. She points her finger at me. 'I warned him, Daddy,' she shrieks. 'I told him not to mention football.'

There's a sudden silence. The blood's stopped raging and crashing through my veins. 'Football?' I say.

'Le football?' says Jean-Claude.

I stare blankly at the French Exchange. He stares blankly at me. I raise my eyebrows. He raises his shoulders and shrugs.

'We do not fight over ze football,' says Jean-Claude.

'Football? What sort of hooligan d'you take me for?' I fling.

'We fight over food,' says Jean-Claude.

'Not over food,' Sarah corrects, 'with food.'

'OVER food!' roars Jean-Claude.

'Yeah – OVER food!' I yell.

We eye each other. Strewth – what a mess he's in. Ketchup's dripping down his chest, like he's slit his throat. Bits of Ric's potato salad are sticking to his hair and T-shirt, like a giant's sicked up on him.

I can feel a stupid grin starting to spread across my face. I can't help it. He can kill me if he likes. Can't stop myself . . .

'Ah! Ah! Ha Ha!'

He's laughing at me! We're laughing at each other!

Everybody's looking dead mystified. Apart from Sarah's dad and Sarah.

'That explains it, then,' says Sarah's dad. Like there could be an excuse for our antisocial behaviour. 'You'd better go inside, lads, and get cleaned up.'

He sees I'm looking puzzled. 'Didn't you know?' he says. 'Jean-Claude's dad's a top French chef.'

# Sandi's sauce

Well, what a turn up. Just when I'm thinking of becoming a chef myself, here I am in Sarah's bathroom all matey-like with the son of a top French chef.

Jean-Claude tells me he's going to follow in his dad's footsteps. He tells me about all the dosh you can earn. And he says girls really go for a chef – just as I'd thought. Says they just throw themselves at you, begging you to cook them your signature dishes. Not all that surprised, actually. 'Cos if my mum's cooking's anything to go by, bet most of 'em have never tasted a first-rate nosh-up in their entire lives.

Hmmm . . . Maybe I *should* become a celebrity chef myself, instead of a pilot? Can't wait to get home now and have a word with Mum about getting in some special ingredients. Like sun-dried tomatoes and anchovy paste. Then I can practise concocting my own signature dish.

Jean-Claude and I are getting on really well. So well, we don't notice the time passing. Suddenly I hear somebody calling up the stairs. It's Ric.

'My mum's arrived. Come on down. Gotta go.'
He sounds dead ratty.

We find Sarah's sulking. She says I owe her dad
for six finger rolls and a squeezy bottle of tomato
ketchup. And she'd never have invited me, if she'd
known.

Oh, and by the way, she's no longer speaking to
me.

Ric's scowling. He's shouting at me to get a move
on. His mum's not got all day.

Oh, and by the way, he's no longer speaking to
me, either. Says it's on account of my terrible and
unforgivable treatment of his potato salad.

'Oi! D'Artagnan. Or should I call you hot-
Dogtanian?'

It's Sandi – who else?

Big sigh. 'What now?'

'You're going without this.' She's holding out my
mum's rustic basket.

'Oh – yeah. Cheers,' I mutter.

I take it. Then I notice something, sitting in the
middle of the wilted vine leaves. It's one big, fat,
juicy strawberry, winking at me, like a jewel. It's the
whopper.

'Where'd this come from?'

'You should know. Tesco's, at a guess. Or was it the Costa –'

'OK,' I cut in. 'Don't start on that again.'

'I saved it for you,' she says. 'Hid it under a plastic cup.'

'Hey – that's decent. Thanks, Sand.'

'Mates?' she says.

'Yeah – can always rely on me, Sand,' I say, in a rush of gratitude.

'Oh, good,' she says. ' 'Cos I need a big strong lad to help me carry Archie and his equipment to school tomorrow morning. Gotta do a talk. I'm doing Keeping Parrots. Only Mum's car's out of action. Thanks, mate. Thanks a bundle. See ya outside our house at 8.15 am on the dot. Don't be late. Ciao!'

Ric honks his mum's car horn. He waves a fist at me. While I'm distracted, Sandi strides away. She kicks at a pebble with her big Nike Airs.

'Stuff yer stupid, moth-eaten parrot,' I yell after her. 'They used to burn females like you at the stake,' I add.

She doesn't bother to turn round. She just wiggles her butt and wafts me a wave, over her shoulder.

Girls. Grr! You can't trust ANY of 'em.

Ric's still giving me daggers. Good. Glad I'm not the only one who's smarting.

At least he doesn't suspect I was fancying my chances of a date with Sarah. Boy, would he get some mileage out of that, if he knew.

'Have a good time, boys?' says Ric's mum, the way mums have a habit of doing when you're slouching long-faced and dead silent in the car.

'Yeah.' Ric and I both grunt together. (Never hint that anything can have gone wrong. Ric's smiling mother's capable of transforming into a female member of the Gestapo at the bat of an eyelid.)

Don't know what Ric's moaning about, actually. What's a bit of salad matter? *He* got to chat up a girl. I didn't. Come to think of it, wonder why he feels the need. Maybe Carrot-top's not much to look at, and he's not letting on. Still, he has got a girlfriend, whatever she looks like. I flipping well haven't.

Lucky escape from Sarah, though, I tell myself. Lucky escape, mate! That scornful look she does could shrivel any bloke's pizzazz.

Funny thing about this girlfriend caper. When it dawns on you you've not got your sights on anybody anymore, things don't half seem to go flat. Must be some girl out there who'd like to go out with me. But how do you interpret the signals? That's the problem.

# Chapter 3

# Make-over mode

# Launch pad

Brrring-brrrring, brrrring-brrrring . . .

'Hi, s'Ric. Get over here, can you? Need some advice.'

'Carrot-top's never gone an' dumped you, has she?' I exclaim, my voice shaking with excitement.

'Nah. Just get over here.'

Click. He's gone.

Seven seconds!

'So – what d'ya honestly think of my pad?' says Ric. He's sprawling across his bed with a sulky expression on his face. 'Go on – give it me straight.'

I glance around Ric's room. I puff out my cheeks and shake my head. 'Dunno. Looks like it usually looks. You know – a tip.'

Ric's room's smack opposite the bathroom. He says when anybody from outside his family wants a pee (apart from me, his best mate) his mum shoots off upstairs and shuts his door before she'll let them up. There's this 'appropriated' shop sign on the door. It says, jokingly, NO FOOD OR DRINK TO BE CONSUMED ON THE PREMISES. And below it there's a Gary Larson cartoon. The one saying, 'Gee Mum! Andy was just showing us how far he could suck his lips into the bottle!'

Ric's room. His creation. His world.

'My God – yeah – what a TIP.'

'My entire past's here,' sniffs Ric. 'In this room. It's living history, this is.'

'Yeah,' I say. I'm really warming to the subject now. 'There's artifacts here dating right back to the cradle. Decor dating from circa age eight!'

'Can't let Carro see it, can I?' he says. 'You know, when her parents bring her over in August.'

'Ah – right! Yeah.' I see his problem. 'Not exactly a shining example of style and sophistication, is it? Interior design-wise, Ric, you've been suffering from arrested mental development since primary school. This's not the pad of some trendy, go-ahead teenage guy – it's more like a psychiatrists' theme park.'

'So if my mum says yes, will you help me redecorate it?'

Ah – so that's what he's been leading up to.

'Suppose so.'

Wish I'd known what I was letting myself in for.

'Mo-om,' bleats Ric. 'You know my room . . .'

'You mean that fetid tip you sleep in?'

'Yeah. I'm fed up with sleeping in a mess.'

'Heaven be praised. The vacuum cleaner's in the cupboard. Polish and dusters are under the sink.'

Ric looks round at me for support.

'D'you realise, Mrs Cooper, your son reached teenage status nearly two years ago, but he's still got Power Rangers on his walls and Spiderman on his duvet?'

'And what does he have under his bed? Answer me that. Enough fluff to stuff a mattress. Mouldering socks, mugs turning green and hairy . . . What does he have in his drawers?'

'What I do in the privacy of my own drawers is my concern,' Ric chimes in, with a rare shaft of wit. 'But if my room got redecorated . . . In a style to suit my personality more . . .'

'Heaven help us,' mutters his mum.

'Strewth!' I exclaim, forgetting whose side I'm on.

'Daa-d,' he bleats.

Mr Cooper's just got in. He doesn't like hassle. He doesn't like arguments, especially after a hard day's work. Above all, Ric's dad knows how to get down to basics.

'OK, son,' he sighs. 'What's it going to cost? And can you get it done this weekend, while I'm not here?'

## Which funny side

'So – what d'you reckon we should do with my room?'

'How should I know?' I groan. Honestly, in the ideas department, Ric's never likely to get further than the substitutes bench. 'It's your room and she's your girlfriend.'

'Do I detect a spark of jealousy?' he purrs.

'Get lost.'

'Tell you wha'. When an' if you finally find your Ms Perfect, I'll help you do your room. Not that I've seen you making much progress in the girlfriend direction,' he needles.

'There's plenty of time,' I snarl. 'Plenty. We don't *all* rush in and snap up the first goods on offer, like you. I'm still shopping around. And talking of Ms Perfect, what's she look like, this Carrot-top? Got a photo?'

'Er – no,' says Ric. 'But she's sending one and you're gonna be dead jealous. An' anyway, what you on about – you'd have snapped up Bec-ky. Like a shot.'

'You put the kibosh on that one, mate. But now I happen to think you did me a favour. Becky's a frump. And a killjoy. I'm looking for something snazzier. And in any case, don't you remind me about my T-shirt – not if you want my help. Not if you want to live.'

'On the subject of girls, I'm thinking of asking Sandi round to give us a hand,' Ric says.

'Sandi? Do us a favour,' I groan. 'I'm not talking to Sandi. Why're you asking her?'

' 'Cos she's good at Art. 'Cos in those decorating programmes on the telly, there's always some babe involved. An' Sandi's a good sport. Can have a good laugh with her. Not still smarting over that parrot, are you?'

'I am. Only it doesn't matter. Ask her if you like. Suit yourself. She's an extra pair of hands, I suppose.'

Why didn't I just tell Ric, straight out, that I'm seriously thinking of calling the challenge off again?

I've gone right off girls. I've been looking really hard since the barbecue, but there's not one of 'em I'd trust tinkering with my sensitive emotional mechanism.

Even Ric shouting, 'LOSER! LOSER!' in his tinny tones, would be preferable to tangling with girls.

As for Sandi, she'll be lucky if I ever speak to her again after Monday. Can you imagine the sheer embarrassment of lugging a loud-mouthed, over-excited, moth-eaten parrot called Archie to school? 'Take yer filthy hands off! Take yer filthy hands off!' it kept squawking. Her brother Martyn taught it that. I'm just thinking I'm gonna dump the cage on a wall and leg it, when this foul old bird launches into its second party piece. It starts making these noises like a croaky wolf whistle. No kidding. So many girlie heads swivel round, I feel like Leonardo Di Caprio carrying a basket of kittens.

'What else's he taught it?' I hiss. 'Go on – warn me. I think I ought to know.'

'Oh, loosen up!' grins Sandi. 'See the *funny* side.'

Oh yeah? Which funny side? How come girls can always see a funny side, when a bloke's suffering?

'You can have a good laugh with Sandi' says Ric. Oh yeah, Ric? Oh yeah?

## A question of taste

Well, Ric and I eye each other's decorating gear. It consists of old jeans and T-shirts that could get us arrested by the style police. We indulge in a few ritual wisecracks.

'So where's Sandi, then?'

'She'll be along,' says Ric. 'Thought we'd get the heavy stuff shifted before she gets here.'

He holds up one of those heavy-duty bin-bags. 'Anything I want to junk goes in here.' He points with his toe at his dad's old cabin trunk he's got down from the loft. 'Anything I want to keep goes in there. Simple.'

'Yeah – right.' I glance around. 'So what you got planned, then?'

Ric sprawls across his bed, head on his hand and one finger resting artily across his cheek. He droops his eyelids. What a poseur!

'I've done some research,' he says. 'Flicked

through every style and interiors mag I could get my hands on down the papershop. I even looked at *The Art Of Feng Shui*.'

'And?'

'Well, my first idea was to build this wall outa glass bricks. They're supposed to "activate" the space –'

'To *what*?'

'You know – make the most of the light.'

'Yeah, right.'

'Only they cost a bomb. And let's face it, there ain't really enough space in here to activate . . .'

'Ah – so you'll be going for minimalist, then. Clearing out all the junk. Painting the walls plain white. Bit of bare brickwork, eh? Like in trendy loft spaces. How about if I get yer dad's sledge hammer and get to work smashing the plaster off that chimney breast?'

Ric squeezes his eyes shut and signals horror. 'Hold on! Hold on! Minimalist's passé. That's arty-speak for 'out'. It's within spitting distance of being out, anyway. In this mag I was reading, it says minimalist's too difficult for normal human beings to live with. I mean, you can't just fling yer stuff down and forget it. It's, like, kick off yer trainers, drop an empty crisp packet – wham – you've blown the whole effect.'

'So, what then?'

'Well, I read somewhere else it's cool to mix up furniture and styles in a way to suit yerself. Even throw in a bit of bad taste.'

'Only problem with the bad taste is that you've got so much to choose from in this dump . . .'

'The basic theme,' Ric states, ignoring me, 'is going to be Retro. The hub of the design's going to be that 1960s leather and chrome chair.'

'Which chair?' I scout around, mystified. 'Where?'

'That one – under the clothes.'

Ric scoops up a pile of crumpled T-shirts, dead underwear and fossilized socks. Under that he unearths several Coke cans from his round-the-world collection. Finally he exposes the 'hub of the design'.

'That's a circa 1969 Habitat chair. It got demoted to my room when I was too young to object.'

'Funny – never noticed it.'

'Well, it's what they call "mid-twentieth-century

modern". And that's all the rage, that is. My chair's a prime example.'

'Yeah – right. If you say so. So what about the walls, then?'

'Painting over the Power Rangers with matt Caramel emulsion paint. Picking out the paintwork with Cappuccino gloss.'

'Caramel? Cappuccino?' I snort. 'You mean, like – *brown*.'

'Light brown. Only I prefer "Caramel" and "Cappuchino". It sounds sexier.'

I pretend to puke. 'You know what brown reminds me of? And that ain't sexy.'

Ric heaves himself off the bed. 'Remember we're in a race against the clock, if we're gonna get it done this weekend, like on decorating and garden make-over programmes on the telly. So come on, quit yacking – let's get cracking.

Several minutes of frenzied activity later, the cabin trunk's already near full of Ric's childhood keepsakes. Not much in the rubbish bag, though.

'Hey!' I shout. 'Look at this. You've still got your Connect Four. Intact. And – wow! I don't believe it. Your Hungry Hippos. With most of the balls. Tell you what, I'll take them off your hands. Trunk's nearly full.' I tuck them under my arm.

'No way! They go in the trunk!'

'I deserve something for helping you out. Okay, then. I'll settle for the Hungry Hippos.' I put the Connect Four into the trunk. But I hang on to Hungry Hippos like it'll need to be surgically removed.

We eye each other. And it's like we're six again. Ric knows I always wanted his Hungry Hippos. I was a deprived child. My mum always put her foot down over buying expensive, garish, noise-creating chunks of plastic with a higher enjoyment than educational ratio. The Early Learning Centre probably never stocked Hungry Hippos.

'No!' shouts Ric. 'I've not protected that game – balls and box intact – all these years, to give it up now. Tell you what, I'll play you – best of six. For old times' sake. Only, no prizes. No "winner gets to keep the Hungry Hippos".'

'Okay,' I sigh. 'Just best of six.'

Off we go. Clatter, clatter! Rattle, rattle! Shriek, shriek!

Best of six turns into best of ten . . .

It's like we're sorta desperately hanging on to the

last threads of our childhood. This could be The Last Time we play.

Best of ten turns into best of twelve . . .

## It's a male thing

'You're right, Sandi – they are!'

Ric's mum glowers accusingly from the doorway.

Caught in the act. Ouch! Ric and I flinch. We exchange furtive looks.

Sandi's standing over us with her hands on her hips. Her lips are curled in sarcasm.

Oh heck. And I'd planned to be all stand-offish and ignore her. Put her in her place and –

'Pathetic!' she hisses.

She's wearing one of those painters' all-in-one white overalls with smudges of paint on it. It's miles too big for her, so she's pulled it in and tucked it up with a snazzy elasticated belt. Very professional looking. Why didn't I think of that?

'Useless and infantile!' she flings.

'I think this calls for a cup of coffee, don't you, Sandi?' says Ric's mum.

Ric's mum's like mine, always ready for a cup of coffee. Only I sense there's more to it, 'cos I catch her giving Sandi a sly wink. There's some sort of silent communication going on. 'Cos Sandi winks back. (How'd they do it? Wink at Ric and he'd ask me what I'd got in my eye.) Sandi reaches down. She removes us both from the bed with a couple of judo-style, no-nonsense flicks. Like she's disposing of a couple of flies.

'Coffee all round,' she orders. 'Oh, and listen, boys – take your time.'

The door slams shut behind us.

We hover on the landing, like a couple of rejects from the toy factory in that old cartoon called *Super Ted*, stamped REJECT and thrown out by a couple of females.

'It's your room . . .' I mutter.

From inside the room we can hear furniture scraping and the sound of brisk movements. You can already smell organization and efficiency seeping under the door.

Ric shakes his head. 'Better make the coffee,' he mutters. We head downstairs, sheepishly . . .

* * *

Ric and I are sitting at the kitchen table. We're sipping coffee and feeling out of sorts. Obeying shouted instructions, we've put his mum's mug and Sandi's on the landing, outside the closed door.

'You could claim they're only carrying out the traditional female role,' I sigh. 'Nest building.'

'So what are we doing, then? Since when has making mugs of coffee been the traditional male role?'

'See coffee as meat,' I say. But that's a bit beyond Ric. 'Traditionally, women stayed at home,' I explain. 'Sorted out the cave. Heaved a few boulders around. Mucked it out an' cut an' spread the rushes. That sorta thing. All heavy, physical work. Prepared the animal skins. Yuck – pretty foul job, when you come to think about it. But what did men do? Hunted. Off we went at the crack of dawn with our spears. Did a spot of tracking – calling for skill and brainwork. Lounged around a bit, awaiting our prey. Got the spear in an' lugged prey home for preparation by the women. Complained about our hard day's hunting and slept it off.'

Ric cottons on. He nods. 'No hunting to be had this close to the town centre these days, so we provide them with instant coffee instead?'

'Yeah – you've got it.'

We take deep slurps from our mugs, get out a pack of cards, whack in a CD, pump up the volume, and ignore all the thumps and scrapes above our heads.

## Millennium chic

At last they've called us back up.

Ric's room's cleared. Furniture's stacked neatly on the landing. Carpet's gone and floor's hoovered and cleaned.

You'd think they'd be knackered.

'Any chance of a spot of lunch, now?' Ric mutters.

They snort, scornfully. They point at two pots of paint and hold out jumbo-sized paint brushes.

'Get cracking!' they say.

I've got this other theory. I reckon all those slave-drivers you read about in history books were women.

By three o'clock Ric's room's looking brilliant, though. Low-key, laid-back style. Sorta 1960s, but given a millennium twist with a silver stripe.

I'm jealous . . .

'Who says brown's not sexy now, hey?' Ric's crowing. 'Think I should go in for Interior Design? Grow my hair long an' buy tight leather trousers. Whatdja think?'

'Yeah,' says Sandi. 'It's really cool, Ric. Fancy redesigning my room?'

Ha! Bet if I'd done it, she'd have gone yuck, yuck, yuck – can't stand brown. Not that Sandi and I are actually back on speaking terms, yet. Apart from, 'Pass that brush,' or, 'Mind that blob of paint I've just dropped'. She thinks she's so clever, yapping out orders, showing off in that painters' overall. Bossy-boots.

Ric's mum's tickled pink. She'll no longer have to make sure his door's shut before visitors use the bathroom. She's so tickled, in fact, she decides he needs a new duvet cover to replace Spidey. And she says she's seen just the one in town. By Ralph Lauren. It'll be wasted on Ric.

Ric rushes off like a shot and changes into his

best cords to go get it. Only, next thing we know, it's Sandi and his mum who're jaunting off to the shops, while we varnish the floor. We sulk.

'That varnish dries really fast,' Sandi says. 'Just think, Ric could move everything back in and sleep in here tonight, if you get started now.'

Like I said – boss, boss, boss. Orders. Orders. That's all you ever hear from Sandi.

## Watching varnish dry

'You varnish that side,' I say to Ric, when they've driven off. 'And I'll do this side. Then we'll meet in the middle and work down towards the door. Got that?'

We pitch in on our hands and knees. And we've been going great guns for a minute or two when Ric exclaims, 'Eeeeeek!' in his tinny voice. 'Still got me cords on.'

'Better change then. You'll wreck 'em for certain. Once they've bagged at the knees, you'll never get 'em right again.'

Only it turns out changing them's easier said

than done. 'Cos guess what? In spite of my clear, logical instructions, that complete and total prat has started his varnishing by the door. He's varnished us in.

DISASTERVILLE!

Arrrgh!

'Panic not,' says Ric smoothly. He points to his tin. 'It says fast drying. But what about me cords? I ain't working in these.'

'Take 'em off,' I say. 'Central heating's on. Only me here, and I'm working with my back to you, thank God.'

He's got them over his arm before it dawns on either of us there's nowhere to put 'em. The room's completely bare.

'What the fizzing heck am I supposed to do with 'em now?'

I sit back on my haunches and ponder.

'Light-fitting,' I say, inspired again. 'Hang 'em from the light-fitting.'

Actually, it looks really surreal with Ric's trousers dangling in the middle of the empty room. Like one of those installation thingys in an art gallery. We even have a good laugh . . .

It's only later, when we discover we're marooned on a small, dry island, about one metre-square, on the far side of the room from the door, that he starts questioning my 'inspired' suggestions.

'It says Fast Drying!' repeats Ric. It's the third time he's pointed to the instructions on his tin.

If he shows me it again, that tin's gonna end up on his head. Anybody can see it doesn't matter what it says on the tin, the floor's showing no visible signs of drying at all.

We've been stuck here now for twenty minutes, clutching our varnish tins and paintbrushes. So close up I could tell you how many blackheads Ric has on his nose, if I'd the stomach for counting 'em.

'Hey! Think I can see a dry patch – over there.' Ric points with his brush.

He's right. An almost dry patch about the size of a football's appeared in the far corner. We pin our eyes and hopes on that dry patch. Like a sail on the horizon.

Ten minutes later. The patch's neither spread nor multiplied. It's still stubbornly, freakishly, the size of a football. The rest's as wet as the minute we put it on.

I've developed cramp in one leg. I've had enough.

'I'm walking across!' I hiss.

Ric stops me with his elbows. 'In yer trainers? Varnish on yer Nikes?'

I grind my teeth. 'In my socks, then.'

'You can't. You'll wreck it. All our hard work. My floor with your great ugly footprints all over it? No way.'

He's waving his paintbrush under my nose. I get the strong feeling he'll stick it *up* my nose if I so much as set one stockinged foot on the varnish.

I look at my watch again. I point at it frantically. 'D'you realize *they'll* be back any minute? We could still be standing here when Sandi comes back.'

In the middle of the sea of varnish, Ric's trousers are dangling from the ceiling. They're swinging slightly in a draught from the window. Like they're taunting us. That settles it. We *have* to get out.

'The window!' I shout. 'Just one big stride and we could make it. Only way. Down the drainpipe.'

Ric looks down at his skinny legs and purple briefs. 'I ain't shinning down the front of our house like this.'

Hmmm . . . he's got a point.

'You go. Down the drainpipe – in through the front door – back upstairs to our spare room – grab me old jeans off the bed – back downstairs – back up the drainpipe –'

'Stop!' I shout. 'I ain't coming back up. No way.'

'What?'

'Why can't I just open the door and throw 'em across to you, you dork?'

'OK – yeah. Go for it.'

I panic for a minute when I have to let go of the window ledge. But now I've actually made it to terra firma. I'm heading for the front door . . .

A second or two later, I'm back again.

'Where's me jeans?'

'Can't get in. Door's locked.'

'Wouldn't ya know it? There's a spare key, under a flowerpot. Side of the house.'

A minute or two later, I'm back a second time.

'Ahoy there!'

'Where's me jeans you stupid prat?'

'Can't find the key. Any idea how many flowerpots your mum's got? Can't you be a bit more exact?'

Ric can't. He points frantically at his watch. He makes noises like he's being tortured. I tell him to walk across the floor. He threatens to kill me.

'It boils down to two choices,' I shout. 'Sandi coming back an' catching us. Or that Mrs Nosey Parker across the street getting a glimpse of your purple jockeys. Which d'ya fancy?'

Ric's leg appears over the ledge, like a big white slug, searching for a toehold. 'Oi! Get yer binoculars out, Missus. You're in for the sight of a lifetime,' he shouts. Then he's on the ledge. He's on the drainpipe. He's shinning down.

Strewth – a car! Turning into the drive. It can't be . . .

It is.

Brilliant timing, or what?

Ric turns round. He loses his toehold. He slips.

ARRRRRGH!

Ric lies spread-eagled in the front flower-bed. His dignity (well, what he had of it) in tatters. Sandi and his mum hover over him. You've never seen such amazed expressions in your life.

He'll never live this down, I think to myself. Never. I even feel sorry for the stupid prat.

# Booby prize

Next thing I know, Ric's hobbling out of Accident and Emergency with a badly sprained ankle. And he's on a pair of crutches. Looking like he's just been repatriated from a war zone. Playing wounded hero to the hilt.

I'm still feeling sorry for him up to this point. But here's where I draw a line. 'Cos when Sandi sees Ric on his crutches – know what? She turns all girlie attentive on him. And somehow makes out I'm responsible for the whole fiasco. Floor, trousers, sprained ankle – the lot. All my fault.

Well, I'm gutted, I can tell you. All the sweat I put into doing that decorating. And what does Ric end up with? A cool new room *and* Sandi's sympathetic attentions, *and* Carrot-top sending him sickly emails and text messages by the dozen.

What do I end up with? Well, Ric did give me his Hungry Hippos. But that was only only 'cos he said he'd decided to clear out all his childish junk, now he's got this stylish new teenage pad *plus* a girlfriend. He claims a new adult him's emerged.

Oh yeah? Oh yeah? Sez who?

But what's giving me most grief is Sandi. Making out that Ric's sprained ankle is somehow all my fault. Siding with that pathetic prat, instead of me. I can't believe she's doing that.

We've been mates for years, Sandi and me. Well, that's the last time I'll do her any favours.

I think it's about time I taught the likes of Ric and Sandi, and Becky and Sarah a lesson. Big time! They all take me too much for granted.

Maybe there'd be some personal advantages in me getting a girlfriend. I know what people are thinking – that I keep blowing hot and cold. But serve 'em right if I won the challenge by getting a date with the most drop-dead gorgeous girl I could find.

Yeah – how about that? Picture their faces.

Still six weeks to go before Carro comes.

Watch this space . . .

# Chapter 4
# Class act

# Group drama

It's Friday afternoon, a week later. You know what Friday afternoon's like. Nobody can be bothered anyway. Our Drama teacher Mr Moody's having a job getting any spark of enthusiasm out of us. Here we are, at the start of the lesson, sprawling and sagging on our chairs – eyes dull, mouths hanging open. Our brains are already full to capacity with the inpourings of the week, and nicely dulled by a fuelling of chips and Coke for lunch. All our thoughts are geared, one track, to the coming weekend's activities. Mainly, who's doing what, where and with who. But in front of us, Mr Moody's strutting his stuff. He's one of those short-but-muscular types. Casually dressed with his trousers ultra-tight.

'Anybody out there?' he goes.

Somebody yawns. Somebody else's got a head cold and the catarrh gurgles. Otherwise, silence. Moody motors on, regardless.

'Think Soaps,' he says. 'Think what sort of characters, events and situations you get in a Soap. Think themes – come on, come on . . .'

Edward (the class geek who knows all the

answers) raises his hand. Slowly, like a periscope. 'Families, neighbours, crime, money, work, health, relationships –' He lists them in this monotonous tone.

'Sex,' chirrups up the lovely Lyndsey. She glances around with this really coy look on her face.

There's a chorus of catcalls.

'Ah, the *buzz* word.' Moody beams at Lyndsey. 'We have their attention, at last.' (Lyndsey's had the attention of the boys all year. She'd only have to list the days of the week and they'd be drooling.)

There's a bit more banter. Bit more discussion. Then Moody says we're going to invent trailers to our own Soaps. Rehearse them now. Act them out next week. Oh, and we can bring in costumes, if we like. We're doing it in groups. Five or six to a group. One person in charge. 'Right – get into groups and find a space.'

Wish I didn't always get this flutter of anxiety in my stomach when it's get-into-groups time. Straight away, the weaklings start herding together. They always do. The rest of us are looking around hopefully. Trying to catch somebody's eye and get to join a decent one.

Apart from Gary 'Bighead' Grant. He's sizing up the room with his arms folded. Like a sergeant taking his pick of the raw recruits. He's brilliant at this sorta thing. And doesn't he know it. What I wouldn't give to beat the pants off Gary Grant.

Ric comes over and joins me. I start to knot up. Great. My team consists so far of me and a nitto.

Then Sandi comes across. She's joining Ric, I presume. I scowl, but let her stay. She can act a bit. And has an idea or two, sometimes.

Lyndsey's been keeping aloof. She's watching the groupings carefully. Lyndsey's a member of our local theatre's Junior Drama Group. She appeared in the Christmas pantomime as Dick Whittington's cat. She thinks that puts her a cut above the rest of us. She's right, of course.

Then I see Gary Grant flashing her a green light.

Lyndsey starts homing in on him.

Only just as she's walking past, Sandi whips out a hand and grabs her by the arm. In one flick of Sandi's wrist, Lyndsey's in our group! She looks about as comfortable as a Mary Poppins who's strayed into Fagin's den. But nobody argues with Sandi.

Wow – Lyndsey's in *my* group!

Now I'm eyeing Edward. It's not escaped my notice that Edward always comes top of the class in any subject that requires a brain. Hmmm . . . He could come in useful . . . I move in fast and stake my claim, just ahead of Gary 'Bighead' Grant.

That's it, then. Me, Lyndsey, Sandi, Ric and Edward.

I sigh with relief.

## Soap and Glori

'Tyneside!' Ric kicks off. 'Let's set our Soap on Tyneside. Ah cun doa Gazza, mon.' He starts to sing *Fog On The Tyne* in this really feeble accent.

'Liverpool's easier,' says Sandi.

'Nah – overworked,' I sneer.

Sandi pokes her tongue out at me.

'Surrey,' clips in Lyndsey. We stare at her. 'A good middle-class Soap. Well, why not? Be different.'

'West Country . . .' drawls Edward. 'The lanes be choked up wi' them thar grockles . . .'

'Bo-oring,' yawns Lyndsey.

'Brummie!' I cut in. 'Am yow gooin' down yower 'ouse?'

'Nobody likes the Brummie accent,' pipes up Edward. 'It's the least popular of all the accents. In a poll the BBC did once, even people *from* the Midlands said they didn't want a new Soap set there.'

I eye Edward with interest. Where does he get these facts?

'We'll prove them wrong, then,' I say. 'Now, who else can do Brummie, apart from me?'

'I only know Geordie,' says Ric, turning sulky.

'So – you can have a non-speaking part,' shrugs Sandi.

'Now, about the actual location . . .' I say, moving them on.

There's even more arguing about this.

At last we reach an agreement. A small row of shops next to a church. The hub of the action's going to be a fish 'n' chip shop called – my inspired suggestion – 'Ye Cods!' Plenty of scope for puns, I point out.

We get a bit sidetracked by puns – 'your plaice or mine?'; 'got a chip on your shoulder?'; 'I fish I could . . .' You can fill in the rest yourselves. Then we decide on characters.

Sandi's going to be Glori, an abandoned housewife who's hitting the bottle in her flat above 'Ye Cods!' Lyndsey says she can't wait to get her teeth into the part of Shazza, the chirpy chick who runs The Kandy Box next door. (Wow – I can't wait for that, either.) Edward's the wholesale deliveryman, Dan. Ric's a non-speaking customer who leans on the counter. I'm doubling as director and Harry Batters, the owner of 'Ye Cods!'

So far, so good.

The storyline's simple. Glori learns that her husband Barry's deserted her for her long-lost twin sister. Harry Batters gets a phone call to say his son's on his deathbed in New Zealand. He decides to fly out to him. But who'll keep the fishes frying while he's gone, and keep an eye on Glori? Shazza has a brainwave – Glori can run the chippy. But will Glori buckle under the responsibility? Will she be able to keep her hands on the fish fryer and off the bottle? And what'll happen when Deliveryman Dan starts redirecting his special orders from Shazza to Glori . . . ?

Then Lyndsey has this really brill idea.

'Let's set it in the 1980s. Then we can all dress up really naff.'

'Legwarmers!'

'Shoulder pads!'

'Stonewash jeans!'

'Punk hair!'

Even Ric, the non-speaking customer, gets enthused. He punches the air. 'Yeah! Yeah! My dad's got a pair of maroon '80s trousers and some incredible white Italian slip-ons in his wardrobe. They're so naff, I can't wait to get 'em on.'

Edward raises a finger. 'Er, shouldn't a Soap mirror present-day life?' he frowns. 'Shouldn't it pick up on current issues, like global warming and pollution of the seas and depletion of the cod stock by overfishing and –'

'Well, yeah,' I agree. 'I guess maybe it should, but the 80s is more –'

'Original,' says Lyndsey.

'Fun,' says Sandi.

'We'll put more effort into it if we're enjoying it,' argues Ric. 'Hey – I'll borrow a Bananarama CD off my mum. We can play that for the theme music.'

A chorus of, 'Yeah! Yeah!'

Edward looks a bit sick.

But Lyndsey flashes me this lovely, big smile.

Wow!

Ding-dong!

Lyndsey . . . ?

I'll let you into a secret. Right now, I'm feeling reckless enough to make a move on Lyndsey.

Wow – Lyndsey. That'd show 'em. What if I won Ric's challenge with Lyndsey?

## Ric delivers

It's the following Wednesday. I've persuaded my group to meet in the form room at lunchtime to do a dress rehearsal for our Soap. I'm determined we're gonna out do Gary Grant on Friday. And for once, with Lyndsey on board, I think I've got the team to do it. Only, we need a bit of polish.

I do a phone noise – 'Brrrring-brrrring, brrrring-brrrring . . .'

'Barry? Oh, hi! Were am yow?' shrieks Sandi, into her imaginary phone. 'Yer faggots've dried up

. . . Yow've wut? Yow've lef' me fer moy long-lorst twin sister? But I thought she wuz – DEAD!'

'Yeah – right. Okay, Sandi,' I cut in. 'But –'

'But – what?' She challenges me, hands on hips.

'Don't think Brummies say "Hi", do they?'

'So what do they say, Mr Know-It-All-In-Charge? What is Brummie-speak for hi?'

'Er . . .' I click my fingers. 'Er . . .' Why's my stupid brain locked into 'G'day'?

Sandi rolls her eyes and appeals to the rest of the group.

'Try "Awroit",' sighs Edward. He nudges up his glasses. He looks totally cheesed off.

'Awroit!' I snatch the word out of Edward's mouth and make it my own with a triumphant click of my fingers. "Barry? Aw-roit?" Try it like that, Sandi. Okay?'

'Aw-roit!'

'You've got it.'

I turn to Edward.

'Now, you, Edward. Can't you try getting into the spirit of your part a bit more? You're Deliveryman Dan. Think – swagger. Think – sex appeal. Think –

King of the Road. Think – think EDDIE STOBART TRUCKS.'

Edward's very slight and pale. He looks about nine. He sighs. 'Don't you think you're getting carried away? I think you'll find Eddie Stobart trucks are designed for long-distance hauls on motorways. Eddie Stobart does not, to my knowledge, deliver to suburban sweetie shops.'

'Oh, sucks to your knowledge, Edward.' I grind my teeth in frustration. 'Look, can you do sexy, or can't you?'

'I'm doing my best. But I'm not going to make a fool of myself.'

Lyndsey emerges from the store cupboard where she's been getting changed. She's eager to show us her 80s gear.

Wow! My jaw drops open. She's wearing shiny lycra leggings in petrol blue, shocking pink leg-warmers, a scoop-necked, faux-leopardskin top, and dangly ethnic earrings that could stun a bloke with a single swing.

Phwoar!

'Come on, Edward,' she says breezily. 'All you have to do is sidle up to me and catch me unawares as I'm bending over the chest freezer, replenishing the ice lollies, and pinch my bum.'

Phwoar!

'Now there's a real professional,' I croak. 'Go on then, Edward – action.'

Edward pretends to scan the room. He spots Lyndsey, bending over, humming to herself and wiggling her bum. He walks up behind her, stiff-legged, like a sulky-faced robot. He pauses. Then he puts out a mincing finger and thumb. And he makes this movement towards her bottom that looks like he's picking off a flea.

'Stop! *Ed-ward*!'

'That's the best I can manage,' he flings.

Sandi groans and covers her face.

Lyndsey collapses on the floor, laughing.

'Just one little bottom pinch and look as though you're enjoying it. That's all we're asking.'

From a far-flung, forgotten corner of the room, there's a movement. Ric hobbles out. He's got a startling suggestion.

'Let's swap places, Edward. You can be the non-speaking customer and I'll take over as Deliveryman Dan.'

'Oh no you don't,' I growl. I know exactly why he wants to change. Exactly what's going on in his pathetic little mind. 'Cos it's exactly what's going on in mine. And I was just going to offer to take on the part of Dan myself.

'An' why not?' Ric challenges.

I turn my hands into ears and waggle them as a reminder why not. ''Cos you can't do Brummie. Said so yerself.'

'Well, oy've bin practsin. So pu' tha' in youwer poype an' smoke i'!'

'Hey – he's not bad,' mutters Sandi.

'Not bad at all,' nods Lyndsey, still giggling on the floor.

'And I can do the swagger,' says Ric smugly. He does this swagger across the room, even though he's still limping. Where'd he learn to do that with his shoulders?

'And I can do sexy.' He hauls Lyndsey off the floor with a leer like Jim Carrey in *The Mask*.

'Hey . . .' titters Sandi, 'he's great. Who'd have thought it?'

'An' I'm a member of the Eddie Stobart Fan Club. Got the T-shirt. So do I get to swap, then?' Ric demands.

'Er . . .' Well, there's no arguing with the T-shirt, is there?

'Hold on, hold on,' Edward cuts in. 'This concerns me as well. And I refuse to swap to a non-speaking part.'

Groans all round. Suddenly they're all appealing to me, 'cos I'm supposed to be in charge. Pressure. Pressure.

I sigh. 'OK, OK. Edward, we'll give you a part as the friendly vicar. Ric – you get to be Deliveryman Dan.'

'YEEES!' Ric punches the air.

Now I'm the one who's looking a bit sick. Still, if our group gets to beat Gary Grant's on Friday, even this sacrifice'll be worth it. Lyndsey'll just love being part of a winning team. *My* winning team.

And while she's feeling well-disposed – who knows?

## Less style, more substance

I've just been stunned by two pieces of incredible news.

First Ric tells me that Sandi's just told him she suddenly finds him 'intriguing', due, he says, to his brilliant performance as Deliveryman Dan.

'Ric,' I tell him, 'you're about as "intriguing" as the ingredients of a dish of mashed potato.' Well, if his best mate can't tell him to wise up, who can?

I'm gobsmacked, to tell you the truth. I credited Sandi with more *sense* . . . And who thought up the part of Deliveryman Dan anyway, eh? Me, Ric – you great pile of dog's doings.

Then, as though that's not bad enough, he tells me Lyndsey's got a date after school. With – would you credit this – Gary 'Bighead' Grant.

How come girls keep dating idiots and bigheads, and not me?

This is the pits.

Geography homework tonight. We're starting this new project. Half a rainforest must've been chopped down to provide us with all these stapled sheets of instructions. Can't make head or tail of 'em. Probably could if I spent all evening sussing them out, but I've come up with this brilliant, time-saving idea. I'll ring my new mate-with-a-brain, Edward. He's bound to know.

Brrring-brrring, brrring-brrring . . .

'Hello. Speak to Edward, please?'

'No. Sorry. He's doing his homework. He doesn't like to be disturbed when he's doing his homework,' says Edward's mum.

'This is homework,' I mutter.

'Sorry – *who* is this?'

I sigh. 'I'm ringing to discuss homework. We're doing a geography project.'

'Oh – that. Just a minute – I'll ask him.'

I drum my fingertips impatiently. I could probably get through to the Prime Minister faster than this.

'Well? What?'

'Ah – Ed-ward . . . Er . . . About this geography project . . .'

'Yes. What about it?' demands his tight little voice.

'Well, I was wondering . . . I thought we could, like, sorta discuss it.'

'No. Sorry.'

'What?'

'It's an individual assignment. Four hundred words approximately. Details on the printed sheets. We all received copies.'

'But –'

'Sorry. Can't help you.'

Click. He's gone.

The gross ingratitude. After I befriended him. Invited him into my drama group.

Ungrateful, the lot of 'em – Ric, Sandi, Edward – Lyndsey . . .

*Lyndsey.*

Hmmm . . . Prefer not think about Lyndsey. Lyndsey and Gary Grant. Urrrrrgh!

I feel gutted.

Next morning Lyndsey texts the group.

> *SOS. CU BREAK*
> *RE. SOAP. LYNDS.*

'So I went for a cappuccino with Gary after school yesterday,' she says.

'Yeah,' I grunt. 'So we heard.'

She shoots me a funny look. 'Just so I could ask him what his group's doing for their Soap,' she flings.

'Oh?' I can feel a stupid grin of relief spreading across my face. She cares about our Soap that much. How about that? Seems I misjudged Lyndsey.

' 'Cos I'm, like, a bit worried about ours,' she adds.

'What?' I'm gripped with anxiety. 'Why?'

Sandi gives me this really browned off look. 'So what d'he say?' she cuts in. Like she's making out I'm going all round the block to get to next door – which I'm not.

'Well, theirs sounds really serious. It's all about drug abuse. It's got lots more substance than ours, if you'll 'scuse the pun.'

'Told you so,' groans Edward. 'Ours is stupid and tacky. We're going to make idiots of ourselves.'

'So why's everybody staring at me?' I splutter. 'We all worked it out – *together*.'

' 'Cos you're supposed to be in charge,' says Ric.

'Yeah,' spits Sandi. 'So what you gonna do about it?'

Honestly, the way Sandi keeps looking at me, you'd think I was Jack the Ripper. Don't know what's got into Sandi these days. She used to take my side. Now she's always leading the charge against me.

'Nothing while you're all staring at me,' I snarl.

'This needs some careful thought.'

Edward puffs out his cheeks and groans. Like he thinks we're scuppered.

'I'll get permission to use the form room again at lunchtime,' I say. 'Meet me there. Straight after lunch. And don't be late.'

That decisive enough for you all, eh?

## Carry on frying

What to do? What to *do*? I bite my nails right down to the quick. And I haven't a clue what happens in double English. Trouble is, I thought our trailer was good. I was enjoying it. I thought it was funny . . .

I stop jabbing my biro aimlessly into my rough book. I stare into space. I'm seeing a vision . . .

Hey? How about that?

Why try to compete with Gary Grant? Why do something serious? Why not make ours really funny? Play it for laughs? A sort of send-up of a Soap?

Hey? How about that?

You're never going to believe this. The group

actually agrees with me. Well, apart from Edward. But he's outvoted, so he's got no choice.

We decide to keep what we've already rehearsed, only we play it for laughs.

Brilliant!

Wow – you should see Lyndsey. Ric's not bad, either. I'm okay and so's Sandi. And Edward, once he's stopped moaning, surprises us all as the vicar. He can actually *do* comedy when he puts his mind to it. Who'd have thought it?

Friday afternoon. The day of reckoning. We've spent the lunch hour getting ready. Not all the groups have bothered to bring costumes. But there's a couple of others who've made the effort, including Gary Grant's lot. I see he's given himself a moustache, and he's wearing this dirty old mac. What *does* he look like?

I'm wearing my DT apron as Harry Batters. Wish I'd thought of a moustache, though.

There's an outbreak of wolf whistling and cat-calling when Lyndsey comes in. She loves it. She does a Barbara Windsor giggle and wiggles her bottom.

Moody calls for order. He sits us down and improvises a stage.

I'm so nervous, my insides feel like they're going through a food mixer.

We're going last.

The first group are so diabolical, we wriggle uncomfortably and avoid each other's eyes. The second and third are mediocre. There's only three people in the next group – two are away – enough said.

Then comes Gary Grant's lot. They're good. Very good, in fact. But serious with it, like Lyndsey said. Gary smirks round at the others in his group. He preens himself. You can tell he thinks his group's so way-out superior, there's no contest.

Oh yeah?

Now it's us. Fingers crossed . . .

We're a riot, from start to finish. The minute they realise we're giving them something to laugh at, we're a hit. And once we realise we're a hit, we start improvising and, like, really enjoying ourselves. And they don't miss a single joke. Afterwards, somebody tells me Moody was laughing so much, he was thought to be in danger of splitting his trousers.

'More! More!' somebody shouts as we finish.

'Encore! Encore!' shouts some spod with a wider artistic vocabulary.

Moody describes our spoof idea as 'very clever and original'. Everybody's congratulating us. Gary Grant looks gutted. Lyndsey, Sandi and Ric are as thrilled as I am. But Edward looks a bit ruffled by all the praise. Like he thinks it's all beneath him.

Eat yer hearts out Carry On team!

## Carry on trying

At the end of the lesson, there's this big bonus. Lyndsey bounces up to me, and guess what? She flings her arm round my neck and gives me this huge hug. In front of Gary Grant and everybody. Like a footballer who's celebrating with his manager when they've just won the World Cup.

Wow!

'Go for it,' urges this voice in my head. 'Go for it. Ask her out now. She's so thrilled, she'll not want to spoil the winning moment by refusing you. Well, go on!'

'Er . . .' I croak. 'Er, Lyndsey, I, er . . . I was, like, wondering –'

'Yeah?'

'Would –'

Only just at that crucial second – wouldn't you know it – Sandi barges up.

'Oi!' she says. 'We did alright, didn't we?'

Heaven help us.

'Yeah, Sand,' I mutter.

'Thanks to Lyndsey.'

'Er, yeah . . . Thanks, Lyndsey . . .' What about me, eh?

Push off, Sandi. Push off! If you don't push off now, the moment of triumph'll be gone. I'll never again find the courage to ask Lyndsey out.

But Sandi totally ignores the 'go boil your head' looks I'm shooting her.

'Come on, Lynds,' she squawks, 'let's go get changed back, shall we? Or you'll miss your coach.'

And she puts her arm round Lyndsey's shoulder and steers her towards the girls' loos.

Arrrgh!

And Lyndsey doesn't bother to ask me what I was

going to say. She doesn't even give me a backward glance.

But Sandi does. She flings me this really mean look, over her shoulder.

Robbed! Am I destined never to achieve girlfriend status?

# Chapter 5
# Strutting my stuff

# What's eating Sandi?

Brrring-brrring, brrring-brrring . . .

'Hi. It's me, Sandi.'

My brain springs into defence mode. Now what's she gonna lob at me?

'Oh? What?' I snap.

'Well, some of us girls went to see Moody. We asked him if we can have a Miss Year Nine Drama Queen Contest for our last lesson of term. An' guess what? He said yes. So you boys have to dress up in drag and –'

'Stop!' I thunder. 'Say no more. Answer's no. No way am I dressing in drag –'

'Spoilsport.'

'Yeah, yeah.'

'You had fun when we did the Soap last week.'

'That's different. I was playing a bloke an' wore my DT apron. No problem. But dressing up in drag's just to give you girls a giggle, innit?'

'You're getting, like, really boring. Know that?'

'Yeah, yeah. An' you're getting to be a real grouch. Know that?'

'And I suppose you know you're making a fool of yourself – chasing all my friends.'

'I beg your pardon?'

'You heard.'

'S'none of your business.'

'You can say that again.'

Click. She's gone.

Girls! I was right in the first place. Lay off the lot of 'em. Should have known better than to let Ric get me involved.

Girls are just TROUBLE – gift-wrapped.

And that Sandi more than most.

Now she's got me wondering if they're all talking about me behind my back. And if they are, is it better to be talked about by girls than not talked about?

## Icon? You can

Lunch hour, a day later. I'm sitting on my own at a table in our school dining-hall, doing homework for next lesson. Trying to suss out the meaning of a paragraph from *Romeo and Juliet*.

This girl-person called Mel, who's in my class for Drama (played the drug dealer on Gary's team), parks herself opposite me. I glance up from my book

and ham sandwich and frown at her. Mel wouldn't
normally join me. She obviously wants something.
Can't she see I'm busy?

'Good book, is it?' she says.

'Yeah. S'Shakespeare. Got it next lesson. Gotta
get this read.' Hint, hint.

'What's it about, then?'

I sigh. How d'you sum up the plot of *Romeo and
Juliet* in two snappy sentences, so a bird who's bra
size's reputed to already be bigger than her IQ can
understand it? Don't want to get on the wrong side
of Mel, though.

'Hmmm . . .' I close my eyes. I roll a piece of
gristle thoughtfully against my teeth. I search my
brain. 'Hmmm . . . Well, it's a Tragedy. An' it's got
these two rival gangs in it an' –'

'On the subject of blokes in tights . . .' she says,
shutting me up with the subtlety of a Chieftain Tank.
I snap my eyes open. I see she's baring her teeth in
one of those smiles that never reach her eyes.

'Sandi tells me you're refusing to take part in the
talent show, end of term. That right?' Ah, so that's
why Mel's thrust her presence on to me – The
Female Mafia's at work.

'You mean refusing to dress up an' strut my stuff in the Drama Queen Contest?' I say. I intend to stand my ground on this. But I'm edging my extremities out of easy reach of twisting, booting or crushing, to be on the safe side. Mel's reputation as a 'heavy' is *awesome*. 'You've heard right. I *do* refuse.' That's telling her.

'Ah, it's, like, changed, though.'

'Er – what?'

'Changed.' She shrugs her beefy shoulders. 'We're making it a sorta talent show instead. What you lads have to do now is dress up as a Female Icon like, like Madonna or Boadicea. An' you have to do a little performance, 'stead of just poncing around. So we'll be judging you on your talent, 'stead of just your sex appeal. We thought it might make it more acceptable. OK?'

I stare at her. I start choking on the piece of gristle. She puts out a hand to pat me on the back. I duck.

'Oh, an' we've decided to raise money for CHARITY. All money raised in the Female Icon Contest goes towards providing a Teddy Bears' Picnic. It's for the deprived kiddies in St Thomas's playgroup. Them what helped some of us out last term by listening while we read out our children's stories. Our thank you to the KIDDIES.

'G-great idea . . .' I stammer.

'Mine,' says Mel.

'And I'd be happy to cough up a financial contribution,' I lie.

Mel's smile turns deadly. She leans across the table and flips my book shut.

'Stuff yer financial contribution,' she says. 'It's yer BODY we want.'

I feel like my stomach's just done a bungee jump. I glance around for a way of escape. But I've sat myself in a corner. And somehow the table seems to have got nudged just that little bit nearer since Mel parked herself opposite. Like a great mountain, she's got me trapped.

'No bodies equals no performance. No performance equals no money equals no picnic equals no FUN.' Wow, that's quite a clever line of reasoning, for Mel.

'But you don't need me,' I wriggle. 'There's loads of others who really enjoy doing that sorta thing.'

'Yes we do,' she states, not blinking. 'One of you

backs out, they'll all back out. Wouldn't want to deprive the KIDDIES, would ya?'

'Well, er . . . No – no,' I squirm. Boy, do I squirm.

'So, like – will ya or won't ya?'

'Well, I . . . Er . . .'

'Look, I haven't got all day. We'll take that as a YES, shall we?'

'Er . . .'

'Great.'

And suddenly this sheet of paper and this biro have materialized in front of Mel. Her pen's poised over the list. 'So, who d'ya think you'd like to be, then?'

And just as suddenly, Sandi and Natasha have appeared behind her. And they're all running these calculating eyes over me.

'Stop! I haven't a-greed,' I bleat. I turn on Sandi and Natasha. 'Friends? Traitors!'

'How about Cleopatra?' Sandi mutters. 'He could do a sand dance. Then whip out his asp an' kill himself.'

There's this crescendo of female cackling. A foretaste of what's in store at the ghastly event itself. Unless I can find some clever way to thwart 'em.

I groan. Was there ever a time when girls were sweet and innocent? And a bloke's body was nobody's business but his own?

'What's his legs like?' asks Mel. 'Could he do tights, d'you reckon? Or is he more a long skirt and flash of frilly drawers type?'

'That's enough,' I snarl. 'Don't push yer luck. Go pick on some other poor idiot an' leave me to finish my homework. I'll sort out my own form of female impersonation, thank you.'

'OOOOH-ER – hark at 'im!' laughs Mel.

'OOOOH-ER!' they all chorus.

'Look – there's R-Ric,' I stammer in despair. 'Go pick on him.'

They do.

Phew . . .

I feel a slight sense of cowardice and betrayal, as I watch them surround him. But suddenly, Ric's laughing. He starts waving his arms around, like he's describing some sort of female corseting. And Mel starts scribbling delightedly on her list. He's sold out to the enemy. Collaborator.

Next thing I know, they're all putting their heads together. Then they turn and glower in my direction. And Mel holds up the list and points at it. She makes a rude gesture with her biro, leaving me in no doubt what fate awaits me, if I fail to turn myself into a female icon . . .

'Mo-om,' I say. 'Does Uncle Graham still have that old flying helmet and goggles? And the leather flying jacket?'

Mum looks me up and down. She's trying to work out my motives.

'Might have. Why?'

'D'you think he'd let me borrow them?'

'Might do – why? Not reading *Biggles Flies Again*, are you?'

'No. Fact is, I've come up with this really clever idea for taking part in that Female Icon Contest. Without having to make a fool of myself. I'm gonna be Amy Johnson, first woman to fly solo to Australia. Female-Flying-Ace Icon. And not a stiletto heel, brush of mascara or padded Wonderbra in sight! Well, whatdja think? Your son's a genius, or what?' My voice trails off. Don't like the way Mum's looking at me.

'Is that your idea of fun?' she challenges.

'It's my idea of not looking like a prat.'

'Boring!' she flings. 'My son's turning into a spoilsport.'

Second time I've been described as such over this little matter.

'You go as Amy Johnson,' Mum says, 'and I'm not sponsoring you. And I'll tell your dad not to, either.'

'What?' I stagger backwards onto a kitchen chair. 'But you're my chief sponsors. My only sponsors, so far.'

'Exactly.'

Sometimes I forget she's one of *them*. Sometimes I forget my mum's a female first, mother second.

'Mum,' I plead, 'try to understand. Just think how forcing me into fish-net tights against my will could mentally scar me – for life.'

'Oh, rubbish. And who said anything about fish-net tights? Must be other ways for you to take part and be a good sport.'

'Like what?'

'Go spy out the opposition. That might give you some ideas.'

Manipulated at school! Manipulated at home! That's me. How's a bloke ever to get any space to sort out his male identity? And trust Dad not to be around to back me up when I need him.

## Putting on the drag

You'd think they'd keep their icons secret, wouldn't you? No way. Poor mutts can't wait to boast.

Gary Grant's going for in-yer-face-sexy. He's Marilyn Monroe. He's borrowing this silver, strapless, sequinned frock. And he's wearing a blonde wig and as much make-up as he can pile on his face. Oh, and loads of fake diamonds. He's miming to a tape of Marilyn singing a song about diamonds being a girl's best friend.

Ric's being a pantomime dame. He's settled for Widow Twankey. He's going for rude, crude an' outrageous. Big boobs and a hoop in his skirt that keeps shooting up and showing his drawers. He's going for knockabout humour and audience participation along the lines of, 'Oh yes you are! Oh no I'm not!' Says he's bound to win, 'cos yer average fourteen-year-old chick can't resist a bit of smut and a good belly laugh. Suspect he's right.

Sanjit's being a cancan dancer. He's good at gym. He's gonna perform a dance routine with breath-taking cartwheels to the music of the French cancan. There's a 'cheeky' finale where he waggles his bum at the audience, wearing these frilly French knickers. Oh, and he might throw them his fancy garter.

Alex is being a film star from the days of black and white called Marlene Dietrich. He sits astride a chair in a top hat and bow tie and blonde wig an', yeah, fish-net tights. And he mimes to a song called *Falling In Love Again*. That's appropriate, I tell him. Could be Alex's theme song.

Tom's being Queen Elizabeth I and making a speech about patriotism. His mum's making his outfit, only she's a bit worried about getting enough jewels for it. Tim's Florence Nightingale. He's not got his routine worked out yet. But he knows it involves a lamp. And do I know where he can get one? Kris's gone for the obvious. He's Madonna. His sister's making him a set of silver beehive boobs out of plastic plant pots. He's miming to *Like A Virgin*.

And then there's Edward.

He's the only one who's not eager to tell me what

his icon is. Typical. But I have my little ways an' means. Ta-da! He's Mrs Thatcher. Wearing a wig, blue suit and handbag. He's going to deliver snatches from her most famous speeches. Says chirpily that he's very confident. He'll need to be.

They all seem to be taking this contest mega seriously. Worrying, or what?

Another thing I discover is they've all got some female helping them. A sister or mother. Or one of the girls from our class. Sarah's helping Gary Grant. And guess who's helping Ric? Mel! And I find out Sandi's helping Sanjit. Traitor. I could always rely on Sandi to help me. Right from Infants One I could rely on Sandi. Feel really sore about Sandi, actually. She seems to have had her knife into me ever since Becky's disco. And it's not even like I've done anything to her to deserve it.

'They've covered every angle,' I point out to Mum. 'Sexy, raunchy, caring, forceful – what's left?'

Mum takes a slurp of coffee. 'Looks like you're not going to win or even get to be a runner-up.'

'Great!' I groan. Not even a runner-up. My pride's at stake. I scowl. I've still got this old, niggling feeling that a mum should be able to fix things – get out the mental sticking plasters. Write me an excuse note.

Brrring-brrring, brrring-brrring . . .

'Hi. Lyndsey here.'

'Oh. Er – hi . . . Lyndsey . . .' I do a juggling act with the phone.

'Was wondering if you'd like any help with your female icon,' she says.

'Oh?' Wow! 'Er – well, yeah. Matter of fact, like – yeah,' I drool.

I cannot *be-lieve* this. Lyndsey's ringing *me* up. Offering to help. Wow! Wow! Wow! Thought I'd totally missed out on Lyndsey.

'Who're you going to be?' she says.

'Well, it's like this . . . I haven't decided yet,' I confess. 'Every angle seems to have been covered. Don't suppose you've got any ideas, have you?'

'I'll have a think,' she says.

Wow! My cup of excitement runneth over!


'Hang on a mo',' says Mel. She has to shake her biro to get it to work, 'cos the list's propped against a wall. 'Okay. Fire away. What d'ya say?'

'A Music Hall Artiste,' I mutter. I'm cringing inside. Sounds really sad to me. But that's what

Lyndsey's come up with, and there's no way I'd argue with Lyndsey.

Mel's big face swivels round. She eyes me, all suspicious. 'A WHA'?'

'Old-fashioned type singer. Out of the Dark Ages. Before telly was invented.'

She puffs out her cheeks, but writes it down.

'So – what'll you be doing?'

'Singing to a taped accompaniment.'

'Thought you'da' come up with something a bit more – dynamic. Bit more – in yer face,' says Mel. 'Look, why don't yer do Victoria Beckham?'

I keep cool. 'Lyndsey's helping me,' I say, trying not to sound too boastful. 'And I trust Lyndsey's judgement completely. She's borrowing my outfit from the theatre.'

Mel rolls her eyes to heaven and sighs. 'OK. Suit yerself. It's your funeral.'

Never noted for her tact and diplomacy, Mel.

## Playing to the gallery

'Omygod!' Florence Nightingale's peeking through

the curtains. He's groaning. He's looking all pale round the gills. Good thing he's wearing a long skirt, 'cos I'm certain his knees are knocking. 'Have you seen the size of the audience?' I take a peek through the heavy velvet curtains myself. Eeeek! And they're still piling in.

We're in the school theatre. The Female Icon Contest's been turned into a whole Year Nine event. Word's got out and it seems teachers see it as a good way of keeping the troops entertained, last lesson before we break up for the summer hols. Did anybody bother to consult us poor mutts up the sharp end? The participants? Nah.

The whole place's awash with de-mob happy faces. And it's anything-for-a-laugh time, especially if it's at somebody else's expense. There's this really crazy, hysterical buzz out there. More like they're here for a prize fight or an all-in wrestling match. It's that, as well as the numbers, that's put the wind up Florence Nightingale, and sent him scurrying for the loo. It strikes an icy chill through me as well, I can tell you. Heaven help us if we don't entertain 'em.

I chew the ribbon fastening on this stupidly big flower and feather-trimmed hat I've got on. Lyndsey got it me from the Olde Tyme Music Hall box at the Repertory Theatre. I run my sweaty palms over my long, yellow flower-sprigged frock. Came from the same place. I have to face that lot, looking like a cross between a bit player in a costume drama on the telly, and Lily Savage on a bad hair day.

Why'd I ever let you charm me into agreeing to this, Lyndsey? I was putty in your hands. And now I'm going to belly flop out there – big time. And never live it down. Might have to seriously consider going around with a paper bag on my head all summer.

I rush to the stage door. I peer out into the car park. My mum's there in her car. It contains 'essential props' – thought up by Lyndsey, arranged by me. Moody, who's in charge (and on edge) insists my props have to stay outside till the last minute. I fight the urge to slip into American gangster mode and leap in, yelling at Mum, 'Step on the gas, broad! Let's get the hell outa here!'

I take a few deep breaths. Get a grip. Trust Lyndsey. Lyndsey's a professional. She knows what she's doing. She does. She does.

I return to the wings. Pandemonium's just

broken out, 'cos the curtain's about to rise. I'm going on last. Tom's drawn the short straw and has to kick off. Poor mutt, standing there, delivering his patriotic speech in a hand-stitched Elizabethan outfit, to a shell-shocked audience who were under the delusion it was going to be an afternoon of non-stop fun.

Jeering starts. My legs turn to rubber at the sound. Please, God, not me!

'Plebs,' Tom spits, when he finally staggers off. His red wig's all askew and he's looking anything but royal. His amazing outfit cut no ice at all.

'That speech rallied the cut-throat dogs of the entire flaming English Navy in 15 whenever-it-was,' he hisses. 'And this frock's an exact copy of the one she wore on the telly.'

'Yeah, but Elizabeth I had a cushy audience compared with ours,' Sanjit mutters. We try to titter through our tight, lipstick-daubed lips.

Gary Grant's on next. He's been psyching himself up backstage, boasting that the bigger and more excited the audience, the better he likes it. What a show off. He does look terrific, though. Rot his guts. Glam with a capital G. Sarah's done a brilliant job on his outfit. Rot *her* guts.

From the minute old Bighead sets foot on that stage, he's a knockout, I'm gutted to say. Wiggling his hips. Setting the old diamonds rattling. He's even got me smirking. They're clapping, cheering, catcalling, whistling. They can't get enough of Marilyn. Gary gives them a short encore and they still don't want to let him go.

'Follow that,' he flings at Florence Nightingale, as he finally sashays off stage backwards, blowing kisses.

There's a loud clatter as Florence Nightingale's lamp rolls past my feet. With a swish of his skirt and a strange gurgling sound, Florence is heading for the loo again, at full gallop.

Crisis!

Sanjit's supposed to be on after Florence, but he's not ready. Ric's nicked his fancy garter. He's using it to fire saliva-soaked paper pellets into the audience. Marilyn volunteers to go back on again. But everybody starts arguing that that's unfair.

In the meantime, Mel's hammering on the loo door and threatening to shoulder-charge it. You can hear Florence whimpering inside. He shouts he'd rather have Mel pull him limb from limb than face that audience. I feel a bond of sympathy with Flo.

It's Sandi who saves the day. She steps on to the stage herself and announces, 'Is there a doctor in the house? Florence Nightingale's been taken sick.' While they're still laughing, she gets Lyndsey to start up the cancan music. After a beat or two Sanjit, who's now got his garter back, prances on.

He's brilliant. The audience clap out the rhythm as he capers around. He flashes his knickers and does high kicks and cartwheels. You can tell they're really enjoying his act. They even appreciate his skill. But they preferred Marilyn. Sex-mad, the lot of 'em. Sanjit throws his garter and returns to the wings. He's panting and smiling, relieved it's all over and they liked him.

Marlene Dietrich goes on next. They like him 'cos he gives 'em what they want – a good display of male limbs in fish-net tights.

Then it's Ric. Remember how he amazed us when he did Deliveryman Dan? Well, now he's doing it again, as a pantomime dame. Some days, Ric can hardly be bothered to breathe, but he's out there now, playing the audience like Gary Grant. He's prancing around in striped rugby socks, a stupid hooped skirt, a towering wig he's pinched from the Drama props cupboard, and a couple of balloons down his front. He's got that raucous rabble in the palm of his hand. They don't half scream and cackle at his stupid jokes. They even fling themselves into the panto-style participation with gusto.

When Ric comes off, he's sweating like a pig. But he's all tanked up on adrenaline. 'Great! Great!' he's muttering. You get the feeling he could go back on stage and do saucy ad-libs for the duration.

Think it's going to be a tight finish between him and Gary.

Madonna's on next. You can see him trembling visibly and one of his plant pots has slipped, but they appreciate his guts in keeping going.

Now it's Mrs Thatcher. Then it's me. Arrrgh!

Can't think about me. Daren't think about me.

I half hope Edward'll get eaten alive out there. I take a peek before I dash outside to collect my props. Surprisingly, the audience have gone all hushed. Like the headmistress's just appeared on stage. That's exactly what Edward looks like in his big-hair wig and sensible shoes. Small and thin, clutching his handbag. There's an 'I'm not going to stand any nonsense' feel about Edward, like a rod of iron's running through him. He's made a good choice of icon. Think he'll go far, will Edward.

No time to see the rest of his act, I nip outside to the car.

'Good luck,' says Mum, as she hands over the props. 'Break a leg!'

I don't reply. My face is frozen.

## Send in the animals

As Edward strides off the stage, after his performance, Lyndsey gives me the thumbs up. Sandi gives me a push.

I'm on!

I feel a total prat, appearing in front of the entire Year Nine, not to mention an assortment of teachers, in this ridiculous rig, but I pin a coy sorta expression on my face, like Lyndsey showed me, and start strolling across the stage.

I'm clutching a big basket over my arm.

The music starts up and as I launch into my intro, there's this expectant hush. They're wondering what's coming next. P'raps they think I'm all done up with Velcro. And I'll suddenly rip everything off and reveal I'm really Pamela Anderson underneath. Pity I didn't think of that sooner.

Now the intro's over. There's this titter of surprise as I start on the chronically stupid chorus –

> *'Daddy wouldn't buy me a bow-wow,*
> *Wow-wow . . .'*

I encourage them to join in. To my surprise, they do. 'Wow-wow, wow-wow,' they echo, a beat behind me.

> *'I've got a little – CAT!*
> *And I'm ve-ry fond of – THAT*
> *But I'd rather have a bow-wow-wow . . .'*

Time to hit them with a gimmick.

I lead them through the chorus again. Only this time, when I get to CAT I whip the napkin off the top of my basket. I lift out – gimmick Number One.

'Oooohs' and 'ahhhhs' ripple round the theatre. They're for Fluffy, our neighbour's fat, pure white

Persian cat. I hold her up. She blinks sleepily in the spotlight. Fluffy's the real-live version of every girl's stuffed-toy dream. I can tell all the girls are desperate to get their hands on her, but I pop her back in the basket. Sighs of disappointment, but I shake my head.

*'I'd rather have a bow-wow-wow . . .'*

You can feel the air of anticipation as I trip to the wings. I hand over the basket and take hold of a lead.

Enter gimmick Number Two, to a great round of applause.

A Rotweiller called Hannibal.

I'd better explain about Hannibal. He's a Rotweiller by birth, but he lives with a poodle. So he has this split personality. Added to which he's only nine months old. In girlie-speak, he's one of the 'cutest' and 'soppiest' dogs in the entire world.

Hannibal's beside himself with excitement. He seems to think my hat and frock are there to deceive him. But he's a bright boy, Hannibal. He knows it's me. He gives this Woof! of pleasure. He rears up and plonks a huge great paw on each of my shoulders. He knocks my hat all skew-iffy and starts smothering me with big, sloppy kisses. What a ham.

Well, the 'ooohs' and 'ahhhhs' are enough to make you puke. Just like Lyndsey said they'd be. I carry on singing and strolling Hannibal up and down the stage, but he's so excited, he starts twisting himself around my legs. He pulls the lead so tight round my frock, I start staggering around, trying to keep my balance. The audience love this. They start howling with laughter. They think it's deliberate – all part of my clever act. I decide to play up to it. I play up to it for all I'm worth.

When Hannibal and I finally manage to stagger off, there's this big round of applause.

'That was GREAT!' gushes Lyndsey.

She tries to give me a luvvie-type hug. Only my hat gets in the way. Then Hannibal barges between us, and I accidentally bash her with the basket.

'D'you think I went down well, then?' I gasp, breathlessly.

'Oh, yeah. Told you they'd love the animals.'

# Reasons to gloat

There's a minute or two of awful suspense while the panel of twelve judges, selected out of the audience, arrives at a decision. Then Moody steps on stage to announce the result.

> *1st Gary as Marilyn*
> *2nd Ric as Widow Twankey*
> *3rd ME!*

YEAH!!!

I'm overcome with excitement. I plonk the basket on the floor. I hook Hannibal's lead round a table leg. Then I grab hold of Lyndsey and start swinging her round.

'Don't know what you think you've got to gloat about,' snarls a voice.

It's Sandi.

'Sanjit should've come third, not you. They didn't vote for you. They voted for a Persian and a Rotweiller. Not *you* – you smelly, pathetic skunk!'

'Oh, take no notice of her,' sniggers Lyndsey. 'She's just jealous.'

'Yeah!' I fling. This is my big moment. I've just come third, and I've got my arm round the dishiest chick in the whole of Year Nine. I *am* gloating. So *what*? I'm not going to let Sandi spoil it this time.

But a second later, the grin's wiped off my face. 'Cos instead of standing up for herself, Sandi just looks from me to Lyndsey and back again. And she doesn't say a word. She just turns round and stalks off.

Weird.

What's even weirder is, she looked like she was nearly in tears.

'Sand . . . ?' I shout after her.

But she doesn't turn round.

'Oh, take no notice of her,' says Lyndsey. 'Tell you what, why don't you hand over the props to your mum? Then we could head for town and grab a cappuccino.'

Can I believe my ears?

Lyndsey's asking me to go into town with her.

LYNDSEY!

ME and LYNDSEY!

TOGETHER!

WOW!

Ric, you are never gonna be-lieve this. You might have beaten me in the Icons, but now you are gonna be so sick.

'Er . . . R-Right. Better peel the false eyelashes off first, though,' I quip. Then I look up. And know who's watching us?

Gary 'Bighead' Grant!

And he's looking absolute daggers at the pair of us.

WOW!

Feel like I've really hit the Big League, now.

As I'm changing in the Green Room I spot Ric returning his wig to the props cupboard.

'Well done, mate,' I say, generously.

'Some kid out there just asked for my autograph,' he boasts. 'Er – you did okay.'

'Thanks,' I say, peeling off the false lashes. 'Did more than okay, thanks to Lyndsey. And now, as soon as I'm out of this rig, I'm about to do even better. Lyndsey and I are heading for town to celebrate our success with a cappuccino.'

'You what?'

'Town,' I repeat into the mirror, as I try to coax

some life back into my wig-flattened hair. 'With Lyndsey.'

Ric's rouge-cheeked reflection stares at me, open-mouthed.

'Looks like I'm about to win the challenge, mate,' I say, smoothly. 'With Lyndsey.'

'On the level?'

'On the level.'

'Cor!' gasps Ric, and bursts one of his balloons.

## Cappuccino froth

'What was it *like?*' says Ric, when I go round his place afterwards.

'Great,' I say. 'What d'you think, eh?' I roll my eyes and mime eat-yer-heart-out ecstasy. '*The* cappuccino drinking sensation of the century.'

'Can't believe it,' mutters Ric. 'You Jammy Dodger. You finally get a date, an' it's with Lyndsey. One of *us* gets a date with Lyndsey.'

I put on a modest expression.

'Well, at least you've got Carrot-top.'

'So, whatdja talk about?'

'Oh, this n' that,' I smirk. 'Just a bit of this n' a bit of that.'

'Cor!'

Well, yeah – going out with Lyndsey for a cappuccino was, really, like – WOW! Yeah – only way to describe it. Really WOW.

Loadsa wow . . .

Not a *lot* of talk, though, to be honest. Couldn't think of much to say to her. And she didn't say much to me, either. We just, sorta, drank the coffee. Well, she's not exactly the sorta girl that fills you with confidence or anything. Not the sort you have a laugh with . . .

She's not like Sandi, for instance. But then, that's different, 'cos Sandi's a mate. Whereas Lyndsey's *the* wanna-have girlfriend . . .

At least, Sandi used to be a mate. Wonder why she got so upset about me coming third in the Icon Contest instead of Sanjit? I know she was helping Sanjit, and she was right – they *were* robbed. I'm big enough to admit that now. But she never used to be that competitive. She never used to be that flipping argumentative, either.

Used to be able to have a real good laugh with Sandi.

'So, you going to see Lyndsey again?' asks Ric.

'Oh – dunno, really. Her parents are dragging her off to Spain tomorrow. We'll see how it goes when she comes back.'

'Wow, that's playing it cool,' nods Ric, approvingly.

'Yeah,' I shrug.

'Cool.'

Question of me and Lyndsey ever going out again never cropped up, matter of fact. And, strangely, I'm not bothered. I'll let you into a secret. I've got a feeling that going out with a girl like Lyndsey on a regular basis must be more like hard work than fun. Be mad to tell Ric that, though.

I beat Ric's challenge with the most coveted girl in our year, two weeks ahead of the deadline. Who'd ever have forecast that?

Amazing, ain't it?

# Chapter 6
# Big day? No way!

# Diet Coke and sympathy

The day after the Icon Contest, there's not a peep out of Sandi. Did think she'd have rung to apologise. We've broken up for the summer holiday now, so the following day she goes off to Yorkshire for ten days, to stay with her ancient sister, who's married. It's the first time Sandi and I've broken friends for more than an hour or two since Infants One. She doesn't bother to text message me, or send me a postcard, either.

Eleven days later.

Brrring-brrring, brrring-brrring . . .

'Hel-lo?'

'Hi. S'only me – Sandi.'

At last. 'Oh. Er – hi, Sand. Where you phoning from?'

'Home.'

'So you're back then?' I say coolly.

'Yeah.' A groan. 'Get round here, can you? I like, need to talk.'

'When'd you get back?'

'Last night.'

This is more like it. Not back more than a few

hours, and already she needs to see me. Why, though? I smell a rat . . .

'You still there?'

'Yeah, just turning the CD off.'

'Listen, Sarah's still in Marseilles, Natalie's in Bristol, Beth's gone to Kate's and, like I said, I need to talk.'

I tot up on my fingers. Fourth port of call. Thanks very much.

'In that case,' I hiss, dead huffy, 'I suggest you try calling Teen Line, Childline or the Samaritans. You'll find one of them a better substitute for Sarah, Natalie and Beth. Sorry, I'm not plugged into my sympathetic listening mode this morning –'

Click. She's gone.

Good riddance.

Only when I start to think about it, there was a sorta hysterical note in Sandi's voice. Something's definitely up.

I snatch up the phone and dial her number straight back.

'Hi. Sandi? Be round in half an hour. Er – better make that forty minutes.'

*  *  *

The door to Sandi's place swings open before I've
even touched the bell.

'What kept ya?' she snarls.

OK, so it's taken me an hour. Well, you can't just
dash into a counselling situation. You'd be no good
if you were feeling below par yourself, 'cos you were
wearing the wrong gear and hadn't thoroughly
deodorized your armpits.

She grabs me by the arm and yanks me inside.
She's got her hair piled on top of her head and
skewered by a couple of pencils. As she jerks her
head up, she nearly puts my eye out. Bad start.

'Come in the kitchen. And watch where you're
putting your feet.'

I don't need a warning. Their hallway's usually all
spic and span. But today it's full of boxes and carrier
bags. It's like picking your way through a minefield.

'What's all this stuff?'

Sandi just puffs out her cheeks and groans.
'Fancy a Diet Coke?'

'Yeah, thanks.'

'Park yer bum, then.'

I eye the kitchen chairs. Where? They're all

covered in stuff. There's piles of washing, mountains of mags, cookery books, scribbled lists, paper bags from local stores with the goods still inside. I scoop a pile off one of the chairs and dump it on the floor. In a corner, the washing machine's chuntering away to itself. Then it goes into this frenzied, clattering spin, and there's something that sounds like a belt buckle pinging against the glass.

'What's going on?' I feel a bit uneasy. Sandi's obviously in a tizz. Now I find their house looks like a bomb's hit it.

'Not all your stuff, is it?' I mutter.

Sandi rolls her eyes. She aims a vicious punch at one of the piles of cookery books. She snatches up a packet of paper doilies, in assorted sizes, and waves it under my nose.

'Does it look like it?'

She dumps a can of Coke in front of me. Then she plonks her bottom on top of one of the piles of washing.

'It's the lousy wedding,' she snorts.

'The – oh. What? All this?'

She nods. 'Unreal or what? Just 'cos a few relations are coming to stay.'

'Like – wow!'

OK, I know Sandi's brother, Martyn, is about to tie the knot. Mum and Dad and I've got invites. The wedding's this Saturday. But I'd no idea there'd be all this mayhem behind the scenes.

'Should have stayed in Yorkshire. Just look what I came home to. Ten days away and what do I find? Not a home anymore – a raving madhouse.'

I glance around. I take her point. 'Yeah,' I nod. 'Tough. So, whatdya want to talk about?'

Sandi puts on this really dramatic look. She shudders. She blows her fringe out of her eyes . . . She stops.

A zombie-like figure's just wandered in. It bears a passing resemblance to Martyn. He's hesitating in the middle of the floor. Now he's glancing around and looking troubled, like he's lost his bearings.

'Kettle's been moved over there,' says Sandi. 'Instant coffee's on the shelf.'

'Oh – er – thanks.'

'Come for his caffeine intake,' she whispers. 'Stressed up to the eyeballs.'

Martyn tips coffee and sloshes water into a mug. He's looking really rough. His hands are gripping the coffee mug and he's staring straight ahead, gritting his teeth. Looks like he's on a white-knuckle ride – look right or left and he might freak out. Look down and he might be sick. He takes a slurp of the coffee with trembling hands. Then wanders out.

Sandi raises her eyebrows. She clicks her tongue. 'See what I mean? Unreal.'

'Yeah. But you were saying –'

Sandi shushes me. It's her mum this time.

'Er – hello, Mrs Weston.'

Mrs Weston actually jumps at the sight of me. Quite funny. Like I've broken in and she's found me robbing the deep freeze.

'EeeeK!' she goes. 'What's he doing here in all this mess?'

'Drinking Coke,' mutters Sandi.

'Oh dear. You've caught us at a bad time.'

'Mo-om.'

'Sorry, Mrs Weston,' I mutter.

'Weddings!' Her eyes are flickering all over the kitchen. Her expression gets more and more pained as she takes in one heap of clutter after another. 'What a mess. And to top it, there's all Alexandra's stuff she's brought back dirty from Yorkshire, where you'd imagine they don't possess such a thing as a washing machine when I happen to know our Lesley's just taken delivery of a spanking new top-of-the-range Bosch Automatic.'

'Mo-om.'

Now she's spotted a pile of Sandi's underwear. It's lying in full view on a chair. Thinking she's being all sly and surreptitious, she picks up a copy of *Hello* magazine and drops it on top. Too late, Mrs Weston, too late. Next she's eyeing the porthole of the washing machine. Deciding whether she needs to stand in front of it. Jeans only in there. That's okay, then.

Now she's peering round the kitchen again. 'What did I come in for? Oh, I know. There's a bag from Oates & Robinson with a reel of yellow baby ribbon in it, somewhere . . .'

I delve into the pile I heaved on to the floor.

'This it, Mrs Weston?'

'That's it,' she snatches it off me, like she suspects I might be a closet kleptomaniac who's into baby ribbon.

'Now, Alexandra, don't forget. When you hear

the doorbell, it'll be Lorraine. And we'll need you upstairs for the *you know what*. And you'll be a good girl, won't you? Remember all I said about this being Martyn and Lorraine's Big Day and you not spoiling it.'

'Mo-oomm!'

'Good. Because we don't want to embarrass our visitor here with a scene, do we?'

'Him?' mutters Sandi. 'He's about as easy to embarrass as one of them politician blokes off the telly who's accused of sleaze.'

I struggle to hide a grin.

Mrs Weston makes a noise and face like a strangled fish and marches out.

## Frock horror story

'What's all this about, then? Why's your mum worried you might spoil the Big Day?'

Sandi looks shifty. 'That's what I need to talk about,' she says. 'Promise me you won't laugh?'

'Laugh? Would I laugh at a mate's misfortunes? Would I do that? Whatdya take me for?'

'They're making me be a bridesmaid,' she spits out.

I splutter. I laugh. Can't help it. I rock on my chair. I jab a finger at her. 'A bridesmaid – you?'

A copy of *How to Survive a Wedding* bounces off my head.

'Hey – that hurt.'

'Good. Try this for size.' And I narrowly avoid decapitation by *The Bumper Book of Finger Foods*.

'You mean you're going to wear a bridesmaid's *frock*?' I chortle.

'Not even my own choice,' Sandi snarls. 'Lorraine's best friend, Penny Harker, and her cousin Tina were the bridesmaids. Only Tina's gone down with measles. They say I'm the right size to fit the frock. So they're planning to force me into it and make me make a stupid spectacle of myself. When was the last time I wore a frock? Eh?'

'Er . . .' I'm not really into this sorta conversation. Can see now why she needed Sarah, Natalie or Beth. Sand wears a shapeless, skirt-type thing at school. But a frock . . . 'Dunno . . .'

'When I was eight. That party at Alison Friday's.'

'Oh yeah.' Funny, I can actually remember it

now. It was blue. Thought it suited her, at the time.

'So I told my mum, I'm not bridesmaiding. Not for anybody.'

'An' what she say?'

'Accused me of trying to sabotage the wedding. Said she'd jolly well get me into that frock "by fair means or foul".'

'Wow! Guess you've no choice, then. You'll have to do it, Sand.' Mrs Weston strikes me as a woman who'd not hesitate to do foul, not with a wedding at stake.

'Oh rats!'

'Er – what's it look like, then? This bridesmaid rig? Can't be that gross, can it?'

She shudders. 'No idea. But bet Lorraine's gone for something all floaty-floaty, like tulle trimmed with rosebuds. Or net underskirts and sequins.'

'Yeah. Like in ballroom dancing.'

'Promise me you'll not laugh on the day. I mean, if you saw me floating down the aisle looking like a squashed strawberry meringue.'

'Promise I'll keep my eyes on the floor. Make sure I've got a clean hankie to shove in my mouth.'

Bzzzap-bzzzap . . .

Doorbell's ringing.

Sandi starts. She looks dead nervous. 'That'll be Lorraine.'

'Tell you what,' I say, 'why don't you give me a preview? If I've witnessed the frock-horror beforehand, it'll not come as such a shock on the day.'

'OK. Good one.'

Sandi gives a shudder and crawls off down the hallway.

I take a nosey peek. A large, flat box appears through the front door, followed by Lorraine. Lorraine's ranting on about gold and yellow. Must be the theme. Mum's bought me a pale blue shirt. Wonder if that'll be okay? She wants me to wear a tie. Wonder if I should?

There's footsteps coming and going on the landing. Doors opening and shutting. Sandi's mum's exclaiming, 'Well, it fits a treat. Isn't that nice.'

I splatter Coke all over the bag of doilies. I'm picturing the expression on Sandi's face.

More footsteps, coming down the stairs. Along the hallway. I get ready. Think serious. I grip the sides of my chair. Control, control . . . Sandi comes in.

I'm gobsmacked. The frock's yellow. It's long. Wow – it's quite plain, apart from a sorta stupid tail-thing down the back. It makes her look like somebody I don't know. It makes her look eighteen.

Sandi raises her eyebrows. 'Well, whatdja think?'

Well, I ain't laughing.

'It's, er – um – well, it's, like – unexpected, innit?'

'Yeah. Exactly. Quite glam, actually,' she says. Then she starts traipsing around the kitchen floor. Pretending she's on a catwalk.

How can girls do it? One minute they're in scruffy old jeans, bashing you round the head with books. Looking and behaving like they're aged about six. Next they're pretending they're auditioning for Miss World.

'Where's the tulle n' rosebuds?' I frown. 'Cos to be honest, I think this frock's too old for her.

Sandi smirks, smugly. 'Don't you think I look glam?'

'You look like an escapee from a bag of Fizzy Sharks.'

Sandi pulls a face like a gargoyle. Not sure

whether she's hurt or mad – or just saying 'sucks to you'.

Mrs Weston pokes her head round the door. 'Don't you think she looks pretty?' She runs this proud, motherly 'one I made earlier' eye over Sandi. Then she frowns. 'But it might help if you took off your trainers.'

I focus on Sandi's feet. I start to giggle. Sandi joins in. We howl with laughter. Then Sandi picks her skirt up and starts doing this sorta clog dance round the kitchen. Even Mrs Weston starts laughing.

That's better.

Well, sorta . . .

Oh, I dunno. Something's changed about Sandi, lately. You could say we're back to being mates again. Only, she won't just let you forget she's there anymore . . .

## Ding dong belle

I'm, like, really surprised at Sandi. She's let that bridesmaid rig go to her head. You've never seen anything like the way she's done up on the wedding day. Packaged inside a frock that's years too old for her. With her hair piled and lacquered on top of her head. Make-up. Dangly earrings. Bet she cripples herself in those stupid, strappy gold sandals she's mincing around in. Should see the way she's showing off in front of the photographer bloke. Posing all over the place. Thwacking the best man round the chops with her bouquet of sunflowers.

And there's somebody eyeing her up. Anthony, he's called. This smoothy cousin of Lorraine's. He's sixteen, at least. And he's wearing a bow tie. Yuck. Slime-ball.

I've just had my first smirk of the wedding. Sandi's dad's had a toast or two too many. He's just smacked her on the bum, while she's talking to that Anthony, and called her 'a fish called Wanda' – on account of the fish-tail effect at the back of her frock. Should've seen her face.

'Seems you've left your sense of humour at home, Sandi, along with your trainers,' I say.

'Butt out,' she hisses at me. 'And take that horrendous tie with you. It's offending my eyes.'

So much for friendship.

'She might be done up like the bride's older sister, Anthony,' I say. 'But try to bear in mind she's only got a mental age of *six*.' Then I stalk off and start talking to Sarah.

Remember Sarah? Sarah's wearing a nice navy sleeveless frock. Always cool and dignified. Unlike some I could name. 'You look very chic,' I tell her.

'Merci,' she says.

'How's Jean-Claude?'

'Fine. I've just been over to Marseilles to stay with his family for a week.'

'Bet you had some great nosh.'

'Mmm, heavenly.'

Never did get around to concocting my signature dish. Not my fault, though. I've had too many other things on my mind these last few weeks. Plus, Mum failed to encourage me. She never bought the sun dried tomatoes and anchovy paste . . .

## A generation fling

They've hired a band. Sarah and I watch as Martyn and Lorraine lead off the dancing. It's a sorta slow dance they don't seem to know the steps to. But suddenly, it breaks into a Fifties rock n' roll number. There's a stampede for the floor.

I'm just going to ask Sarah if she'd like to join in when – I can't be-lieve my eyes – Sandi's mum grabs my dad and they leap on to the dance floor.

Arrrgh! I've never seen such a disgusting public display in my en-tire life. Mrs Weston's wearing this gross flowered dress n' jacket. It's at least three centimetres shorter than her legs can take. She's taken off the hat that looked like the shield of Boadicea, thank heaven, but now she's rock n' rolling like some teenager who's gone demented. As for my dad, he's doing things with his hips no guy who's turned forty and in a sedentary occupation should even attempt.

'Hey, isn't that your dad?' says Sarah. 'Look at him go.'

I look for somewhere to hide. I spot my mum. Can't she do something? But she's still tucking into the remains of the sherry trifle. She gives me this happy smile and starts doing what I think's some complicated form of semaphore. Only Sarah tells me it's not. It's something called a Fifties 'hand-jive'.

Double arrrgh!

There's this tug on my arm. It's Sandi, with a strand of hair hanging loose. She's pointing at the spectacle on the dance floor. 'Quick – do something!' she yells at me.

'Like what?'

'Bucket of water. Fire alarm. Use your imagination. Anything. I've never been so embarrassed in my entire life.'

'Oh, don't worry,' says Sarah. 'They're just enjoying themselves. It's a generation thing.'

'They're not your mum and his dad,' shouts Sandi.

'If you can't beat 'em, join 'em,' says Anthony, popping up, all smoothy-smoothy at Sandi's elbow. He starts pulling her towards the dance floor. I grab Sarah's hand and we follow them.

Sarah's just left me standing, in the middle of the dance floor. She's gone off in a huff. Says she can't dance with a bloke whose head appears to have been attached back to front. Must've noticed my attention was entirely focused on the antics of my dad and Mrs Weston and Sandi and Oily Anthony.

I go and watch from behind a display of yellow

chrysanthemums. I'm just thinking I might at least barge in between Sandi and Anthony. Only, a bloke with a white beard and white hair beats me to it. He's about five foot nothing and aged about eighty. I hear him introducing himself to Sandi as Lorraine's godfather.

Can't half dance, though, old godfather.

At last, Sandi's managed to escape from the godfather's clutches. She's tottering off towards the Ladies.

I follow her.

'That Anthony's a prat,' I say.

She frowns. 'What ya on about?'

'That Anthony's an oily creep an' – OW-UCH.' Sandi doesn't half know how to inflict maximum pain with those little spikey heels of hers.

As I'm inspecting my new moc-croc loafers to see if she's actually punctured the leather, Mrs Weston comes over. She taps me on the shoulder and starts to talk to me. Her speech is, like, really slurred. It's embarrassing. She's talking *really, really* slowly and *really, really* carefully. Like she's just had false teeth fitted and she's scared she might lose them.

I finally make out what she's saying. She's

looking for Sandi, 'cos it's time for Lorraine to get changed into her going-away outfit and Sandi's supposed to help. Heaven knows why.

Great. That'll keep Sandi away from Anthony for a bit longer. I eagerly point Mrs Weston in the direction of the loos.

'Look at that,' mutters Sandi, just after we've waved the happy couple off on honeymoon. She's flashing hatred. It's Anthony she's glowering at. He's dancing with Sarah and looking like he's having fun.

Thought they might get on . . . I hide a grin.

'And he told me *I* was the best-looking girl here.'

'Yeah,' I mutter. 'Slime ball.'

'And my feet hurt,' she complains.

'Not surprised,' I grunt.

She looks around for a spare chair and plonks herself on it. She kicks off the gold sandals. I warn her she'll never get 'em on again, but she tells me to mind my own biz.

'And anyone who's got vile moc-croc loafers on his feet can talk,' she says.

'Well, I wouldn't expect you to know what's in and what's out,' I sneer.

'*In* where?' she shrieks. 'Timbuctoo?'

I've had enough of her insults. If this is all the thanks I get, it's the last time I waste my superior taste advising Sandi Weston on frocks, fashion – or anything.

Dad comes over and butts in. 'Ahem! Sorry to cut in on the cosy conversation, kids, but it's time we were off, son. Our taxi's outside with the meter running . . .'

## After the party's over

My dad and I are on our way home in the back of the taxi. Dad's enjoyed himself, but I'm feeling tired and sorta bruised. Like I've just been a contestant in a really crazy instalment of *The Generation Game*. I try to relax, but it's ruined by Dad. He's just realised he's totally mislaid Mum. Not that he seems to care much. He's just asked me if *I* know where she is.

'You're supposed to look after Mum,' I explode. '*I* can't be responsible for everybody.'

'Panic not,' says Dad, breezily. 'She'll turn up.' Like it's a bad penny he's talking about. 'Nearly twenty years of marriage,' he adds, 'and I haven't succeeded in losing her yet. Ha, ha, ha! Te, he, he!' He falls around laughing and the taxi driver joins in.

'Enjoy the wedding, son?' Dad asks me a minute or two later, between warbled snatches of a Beatles' song called *Love Me Do*.

'I know I risk sounding like a spoilsport, Dad,' I grind, 'but I can think of a million better ways to pass my time than at a wedding.'

'Oh, but just wait till it's your own wedding, son. Won't be saying that then, hey? Hey?' Dad leers. He digs me in the ribs. He winks at the taxi driver in the mirror. 'Got anybody in mind?'

'Dad,' I tell him, 'get this straight. I'm never gonna marry anybody. Ever!'

'Yo, son!' My dad applauds. He thumps me on the back.

'Chip off the old block,' he crows. ' 'Cos that's exactly what I said myself, when I was your age. Ha, ha! Te, he!'

Dad rolls all over the back seat, laughing.

Do I groan.

Even just thinking about having my own Big Day fills me with dread. It's like, there you are, plighting your troth (or whatever it is you do) to some female. This alien-type who's programmed to think six thoughts at once, and you can reckon at least five of 'em are aimed at getting the better of us males. And while you're doing that, what are your friends and family doing? Boozing. Bingeing. Getting off with each other, and leaping around doing ancient fertility dances, like The Birdie Dance and Agadoo.

It's primitive. They can colour it all in yellow and gold. They can throw in bunches of sunflowers and bottles of champagne. And hand round silver trays with poncey bits of finger food on. Makes no difference. At wedding receptions, everybody reverts to the cave.

Count me out.

# Chapter 7

# The morning after the day before

# Big day debriefing

Brrring-brrring, brrring-brrring . . .

'Oh, er . . . (cough) Hi. It's Sandi.'

'Oh, er . . . (cautious throat clearing) Hi.'

'Give it to me straight – did I make a spectacle of myself yesterday? At the wedding?'

'Want the truth?'

Groan. 'Yeah – go on. Let me have it.'

'Well, if we'd stuck a searchlight on your head, Sand, you could've competed with Blackpool Tower . . . Mickey Mouse ears attached and you'd have –'

'OK, OK,' she snaps. 'Cut the wisecracks. You're saying I got over-excited? You're saying I made an idiot of myself, aren't ya?'

Shame she doesn't appreciate my wisecracks . . . I'd got a few more lined up. 'Nah. You looked, er –' I choose the word carefully. 'Great. You got a bit, er, high-spirited, but shouldn't think anybody noticed. They were all carrying on like they were auditioning for the final instalment of Families From Hell.'

Sandi oozes relief. 'Oh, great. That's what I

thought. Only I needed to hear it. Thanks. Thanks a bundle.'

'S'okay.'

## Scored! But whose game was it?

A second or two later, Sandi's calling me back.

'Yeah? What?'

'It's a really gross scene round here,' she hisses. 'Relations still cluttering the place up – everywhere you look. Polishing off the booze, scoffing up stale canapés. Smoking cigars in the loo. And, know what they're doing now? They've got the photo albums out. Mum and Dad's wedding – Sandi in inflatable paddling pool, aged two – in the nuddy. Know what I mean?'

I sympathise. 'Been there myself, Sand.' I hesitate. A bold thought's just popped into my head . . .

'You still there?' says Sandi.

'Yeah – just thinking.' I chew my lip . . . 'Er, don't suppose you'd fancy taking refuge round ours, would ya?' I say, like, all offhand. 'Could, like – chill out over a pizza n' video, or play a few CDs. Think Mum's got a Pepperoni Paradise in the deep-freeze.'

I notice the knuckles on my hand gripping the mobile. They've turned white. Why's that? This is only Sandi I'm talking to.

She seems to hesitate for yonks. Then, know what she says?

'Is that a date?'

This funny sorta tremble shoots through me.

'What?'

'Are you, like, asking me on a date? Sounds like it, only I want to be sure.'

I swallow. 'I, er . . .' The phone's suddenly turned so slimy with perspiration, I nearly drop it.

'Only I need to know,' she says. Forced laugh. 'Don't want to turn up and find you've invited all my friends as well.'

'What? Whatdja mean? W-would I do a thing like that?'

'Yeah – all the time.'

Suddenly she's bawling me out.

'I invite you to Becky's disco,' she flings. 'Whatdja do? Try to get off with Becky. I get Sarah to invite you to her barbecue – whatdja do? Try to pull Sarah. I get Lyndsey to join our Drama group, so we'd be the best – whatdja do? Make a prize ass of yourself, drooling over Lyndsey. And all Lyndsey cared about was using you to make Gary Grant jealous. Only you're so thick you can't see it.'

She stops to draw breath. 'I don't know what's got into you. You've been really horrible to me lately,' she gulps.

Wow. I'm reeling.

'I even tried going off with Anthony yesterday. Just to get my own back. Whatdja do? Went after Sarah again.'

I'm staggering.

'Hang on a mo' Sandi,' I gasp. 'Let me catch up.'

'And we've been going out together since Infants One. Well, on and off.'

My head's spinning.

'Sandi,' I mutter. 'I can't keep up. Where are we now? Are we on or are we off?'

'Depends on you,' she says. 'If I come round now, it's on.'

'So, ya really wanna come round, then?' I ask, cautiously, like I'm trying out a moon walk.

'You still want me to?'

'Well, er – yeah. OK, then. If ya like.'

'OK then. See ya in half an hour? I'll bring some CDs.'

'Right.'

'Right.'

Phew! Heck! I'm so shattered, I can't get outta the chair. I sit staring at the phone. I've just fixed up a date – with Sandi. Me and Sandi! Wouldja believe that?

How does it feel? Well, when my brain's stopped feeling so numb, I think it's going to feel – great. Wish it had dawned on me sooner that she fancied me, though. Think of all the hassle it would have saved me with the other girls. 'Cos I'd never have looked at another girl, if I'd known. None of 'em's a patch on Sandi. Could even have kept my Flying Fund intact.

Ouch!

Brrring-brrring, brrring-brrring . . .

'Hi – s'Ric.'

'Oh, hi.'

'Guess what?' he says, smugly. 'Carrot-top's coming tomorrow. She can't stop long, though. They're on their way to her auntie's. But if you happen to just drop by our place around two o'clock, you might get to meet her. My girlfriend.'

'Oh, right. Thanks. I will.'

I grin. A great big, cheesy grin.

'Er – alright if I bring my girlfriend along as well?'